Rascal
DOES NOT DREAM
of His
Girlfriend

hajime kamoshida

Illustration by
keji mizoguchi

Chapter 1	Dream of an Imitation Lover	001
Chapter 2	Walking Through the Fog	037
Chapter 3	A Butterfly Flaps Its Wings	071
Chapter 4	Two Lines Running Along, Never Crossing	107

Rascal
DOES NOT DREAM of His
Girlfriend

Hajime Kamoshida

Illustration by
Keji Mizoguchi

YEN ON

New York

Rascal Does Not Dream of His Girlfriend
Hajime Kamoshida

Translation by Andrew Cunningham
Cover art by Keji Mizoguchi

This book is a work of fiction. Names, characters, places, and incidents are the product of the author's imagination or are used fictitiously. Any resemblance to actual events, locales, or persons, living or dead, is coincidental.

SEISHUN BUTA YARO WA GIRLFRIEND NO YUME WO MINAI Vol. 14
©Hajime Kamoshida 2024
Edited by Dengeki Bunko
First published in Japan in 2024 by KADOKAWA CORPORATION, Tokyo.
English translation rights arranged with KADOKAWA CORPORATION, Tokyo through TUTTLE-MORI AGENCY, INC., Tokyo.

English translation © 2025 by Yen Press, LLC

Yen Press, LLC supports the right to free expression and the value of copyright. The purpose of copyright is to encourage writers and artists to produce the creative works that enrich our culture.

The scanning, uploading, and distribution of this book without permission is a theft of the author's intellectual property. If you would like permission to use material from the book (other than for review purposes), please contact the publisher. Thank you for your support of the author's rights.

Yen On
150 West 30th Street, 6th Floor
New York, NY 10001

Visit us at yenpress.com
facebook.com/yenpress
twitter.com/yenpress
yenpress.tumblr.com
instagram.com/yenpress

First Yen On Edition: June 2025
Edited by Yen On Editorial: Ivan Liang
Designed by Yen Press Design: Andy Swist

Yen On is an imprint of Yen Press, LLC.
The Yen On name and logo are trademarks of Yen Press, LLC.

The publisher is not responsible for websites (or their content) that are not owned by the publisher.

Library of Congress Cataloging-in-Publication Data
Names: Kamoshida, Hajime, 1978– author. | Mizoguchi, Keji, illustrator.
Title: Rascal does not dream of bunny girl senpai / Hajime Kamoshida ; illustration by Keji Mizoguchi.
Other titles: Seishun buta yarō. English
Description: New York, NY : Yen On, 2020. |
Contents: v. 1. Rascal does not dream of bunny girl senpai
Identifiers: LCCN 2020004455 | ISBN 9781975399351 (v. 1 ; trade paperback) |
Classification: LCC PZ7.1.K218 Ras 2020 | DDC [Fic]—dc23
LC record available at https://lccn.loc.gov/2020004455

ISBNs: 979-8-8554-1829-3 (paperback)
979-8-8554-1830-9 (ebook)

10 9 8 7 6 5 4 3 2 1

LSC-C

Printed in the United States of America

I'm glad I met you.
That's not how I see things.
My soulmate's no longer out there.
But the love songs we listened to all agree.
We will meet again.
Don't be afraid to get lost.
Get up, fling that door open, step outside.
But the future is not guaranteed.
I'll be alone again tomorrow.
No one to split things with.
This empty hollow in my heart.
If I have to feel like this…
I wish I'd never met you.

    Touko Kirishima, "Turn the World Upside Down"

Chapter 1
Dream of an Imitation Lover

1

One day, Sakuta Azusagawa ran after a wild bunny girl and wandered into a very strange world.

April 1.

They'd boarded a Minatomirai Line express at Yokohama Station, and it wasn't long before it reached the next stop, Bashamichi Station.

They waited for the doors to open and joined the flow of passengers getting off. More people streamed from other doors, and the distinctive brick-walled underground platform was instantly packed.

This was a young crowd, generally ranging in age from middle school to midtwenties. Most were old enough to at least be in high school, though. About equal numbers of boys to girls.

"Everyone's going to the music festival," said Sakuta's companion.

He turned to look at Ikumi Akagi.

"……"

"What?" she asked, catching his silent gaze.

"Just wondering why I'm on a date with you, Akagi."

They'd met up at Yokohama Station, at the edge of the Minatomirai platform. All the way at the front.

"I invited you, and you didn't say no," Ikumi said without batting an eye—or even glancing in his direction.

"I didn't say no because it was you asking," he said, looking forward again.

"Even though you've got a wonderful girlfriend."

Again, her tone stayed even. Her words were likely meant to be funny, but she looked so serious it was hard to tell.

"I know you're curious about that dream, Akagi."

This was the reason he'd taken her up on the offer.

"So is everyone here," Ikumi said. Sakuta could see that behind her glasses, Ikumi's eyes were watching the young people congregating at the escalators.

Nearly all of them were headed to the same place.

A ten-minute walk from Bashamichi Station would take them to the Red Brick Warehouse on the coast, a famous Yokohama tourist attraction and date spot.

Today it would be a music festival.

"Hence the crowds."

Sakuta and Ikumi's theory was proved by the group of high school girls in front of them.

"Can't wait for this festival!"

"The #dreaming thing? Will there be a live reveal?"

"You know it! I dreamed about it!"

"Mai Sakurajima is Touko Kirishima? That's wild! I'm screaming already."

Everyone was waiting for Mai's announcement.

They were excited to see if their dreams would come true, hoping the future would turn out like #dreaming said it would.

Similar conversations were happening behind them, next to them, all over the platform.

The same uncanny dream Sakuta himself had witnessed.

They'd dreamed Mai got up onstage and belted out a Touko

Kirishima song. Then she straight-up said, "I'm Touko Kirishima," and the crowd went absolutely wild.

In Sakuta's dream, he'd slipped out of the concert to call Ikumi. On his cell phone...

Meanwhile, Ikumi had dreamed about getting a call from Sakuta. That's why she was "curious."

"Very Akagi to go confirm things with your own eyes."

"If things do turn out like the dream and I'm not with you, you're the one in trouble, Azusagawa. *You* don't have a cell phone."

Her tone remained perfectly calm.

"Since that's not going to happen, there's no need to worry."

The dream wasn't real.

Sakura knew better.

He knew Mai wasn't Touko Kirishima.

She'd told him she planned to get up on that festival stage and deny being Touko Kirishima, clearly and irrefutably.

The escalator was packed with people buzzing about the Mai Sakurajima = Touko Kirishima theory, so Sakuta took the empty stairs up toward the exit.

Ikumi followed without complaint.

One floor up, at the exit gates, they were met by a domed ceiling. An underground chamber, orange from the bricks all around.

A fancy bit of design, both modern and retro.

The brick motif continued to the concourse beyond the gates, and Sakuta's eyes followed the brick columns up through the atrium. It was stylish, and the vibes meshed well with the station name, which meant "carriage road."

Following the signs to the aboveground exits, they heard the sounds of a piano drifting down from the atrium above. A small crowd was forming one floor up; Sakuta couldn't see much from here, but they were probably staring at a street piano. That was the source of the music.

Sakuta recognized the song.

Most likely everyone here did.

It was a Touko Kirishima number, the song Mai sang in their collective dream.

The person playing that piano might well have seen the same dream Sakuta had.

As he wondered, the college couple ahead of them started talking about Mai Sakurajima.

"She was incredible even as a kid."

"That morning soap? My mom couldn't get enough of it. Always had that red knapsack on—so cute."

"Yeah, I remember that! Really takes me back."

Sakuta and Ikumi heard every word of it. She shot him a glance, probably wondering how it felt to hear people discussing his girlfriend.

This couple had no idea her boyfriend was listening in.

That struck him as funny, and Sakuta had to suppress a laugh.

But a moment later, he caught something red in the corner of his eye.

A floor above, visible through the atrium.

On the passage where the street piano had to be standing.

A little girl in a red knapsack wove through the crowd. She moved quickly, not breaking stride.

"……?"

His pace faltered, as he was distracted by that strange sight.

"Someone you know?" Ikumi asked.

"Knapsack Mai……"

Seen from behind, long hair swaying, just as the couple had described her. That was exactly what Mai had looked like back when she'd been on that morning soap.

"Knapsack……?"

Ikumi followed his gaze, but that didn't clear up anything for her. Not long after, the knapsack vanished into the crowd.

"From grade school. You saw it, right?" he checked.

"Sorry, I didn't." Ikumi shook her head. "Sure it wasn't a trick of the eyes?"

"Didn't feel like it. Gonna go make sure."

A fathomless panic drove him forward. Sakuta pushed forward past the college couple.

"Wait, Azusagawa!" Ikumi called, but he left her behind, rushing up the stairs to the floor above.

No sign of the knapsack kid anywhere.

"Mai Sakurajima was already beautiful even as a child star. The other day, I stumbled across an old commercial of hers online…"

"The car commercial?"

"Yeah, that's the one!"

Near the top of the escalator, some college girls were gathered around a phone.

Everyone was talking about Mai today.

She was the one person on everyone's mind.

"That growth spurt came up quick!"

He wasn't even trying to eavesdrop; his ears caught them anyway.

Then he spotted a red knapsack by exit 6—the one closest to the Red Brick Warehouse. She vanished down the corridor.

"……?"

Sakuta took a step after her but hesitated. Something seemed off.

She was much taller than the girl he'd seen a moment earlier. Not much shorter than she was now. Even the way she walked was more mature.

She'd *grown*.

At least, to Sakuta's eyes.

"What the……?"

His confusion was mounting.

"Find her?" Ikumi asked, catching up.

But he was unable to answer that question.

Arguably, he had.

But that wasn't the knapsack kid he'd originally been chasing after. He'd found a noticeably older version.

Sakuta didn't know what was going on here.

He had no clue how to explain this to Ikumi.

But he *had* seen her again, which convinced him the girl was out there and not just a trick of the eyes or his imagination.

That left with him only one option.

"It really was a past version of Mai. Keep an eye out for her, Akagi."

With that, Sakuta ran off, hoping to catch the knapsack kid. He wove through the crowds, heading to the exit she'd used. Then up the stairs to the outside world.

On the surface, he was greeted by the pale-blue skies of spring.

It was just past three.

Even in the light of day, the flow of pedestrians formed a single stream. They were taking a leisurely stroll down the brick-paved road that led to the sea. To the Red Brick Warehouse.

Sakuta squinted at the crowds but found no red knapsacks.

As he looked right and left, people poured past him. He heard Ikumi running up behind him.

He passed by an old beef hot-pot shop, and a hotel on the far side of the street, then a bridge. He got caught at a red light at the intersection beyond—outside another hot date spot, the Yokohama World Porters mall.

"Uh, Azusagawa," Ikumi said, scanning her surroundings.

"What?" he asked, sweeping his eyes right to left.

"If Sakurajima was here, *everyone* would notice."

She looked him dead in the eye.

And he met that gaze, holding it.

"True. You're right…"

She had a point.

Everyone had been talking about Mai Sakurajima.

If Mai had walked right under their noses where everyone could see—they'd have spotted her instantly. Even if she wasn't her present self, but a little-kid version—she'd already been a famous face since childhood. Lots of people knew Mai now. *Everyone* knew Mai the child star.

There was no way they wouldn't notice her.

"Mai Sakurajima is so cute."

Some college guys at the light behind him were chatting.

"I bought her photo book in junior high."

"The one that sold so fast you couldn't find it?"

"I saw that movie, too. The heart condition one."

"First time I've ever cried in a theater. I even got a donor card."

"Same!"

They all broke into laughter.

The light was still red. Cars were zipping by. Across the street, another group of young people were waiting—and a girl passed by behind them.

Junior high aged.

Barefoot in a white dress.

Sakuta would recognize her anywhere.

It was Mai before he met her. She looked like she had just stepped out of the very movie those college guys were talking about.

White-dress Mai was headed for the Red Brick Warehouse. Every step brought her closer to it.

"Another one?"

His brain was not processing what his eyes were seeing. It came out as a grumble.

"She's here?"

"Across the street."

He pointed to the girl in the white dress, but Ikumi just squinted, not seeing her at all.

The light turned green.

The crowd started moving.

"Sorry, Akagi, I'm gonna run ahead."

"Ack, hold up—"

The crowd that had been waiting on the far side started walking toward him. When the two crowds collided, all he could see were the people walking around him.

Sakuta slipped through and made it across the street—but by then White Dress Mai was gone.

"What is going on...?"

His thoughts crossed his lips verbatim.

"Seriously?"

Once proved not enough, and he muttered again—picking up his pace toward the warehouse.

He didn't know why.

He didn't know what was happening.

But he knew *something* was going down.

And that was unsettling.

He'd seen Mai once—he had to find her again.

Knapsack kid or white-dress teen—he didn't want them running into the real Mai. If they were *also* Mai, then they could not simultaneously exist.

He was almost at the Red Brick Warehouse.

Mai would be performing in this music festival. That meant she was already there.

Scanning the crowds, Sakuta forged ahead.

He found no knapsack kids.

Nor any girls in white dresses.

There had been no further sightings by the time he reached the Red Brick Warehouse.

The two brick buildings loomed on either side of him.

The clearing between them was normally open to the public, but today it was fenced off—and already filled with festivalgoers.

At the far end of the lot, a rock band was playing. The audience seemed to be having the time of their lives, with everyone in the crowd jostling one another. Sakuta could feel the energy through his soles.

This was definitely the music festival.

Sakuta got in line by the white reception tent, aiming for the venue. Two men in their twenties stepped up behind him.

"Girl I met at that mixer went to high school with Mai Sakurajima."

"Seriously? What was she like?"

"She likes bunnies."

"Is that right?"

"Her phone case and hairpin were both rabbit themed."

"That's perfect. She's into bunnies, and I'm into bunny girls."

"In your dreams," his friend said, laughing.

"Wouldn't you wanna see bunny-girl Mai Sakurajima?"

"You're obsessed. This is *the* Mai Sakurajima! She would never wear that!"

They were both laughing now. The lady at reception said "Next" to Sakuta.

As he stepped up to the counter, he spotted two ears cutting through the crowds—bunny ears poking out above the sea of heads. Unmistakably the black ears of a bunny-girl costume.

They bobbed up and down, left to right.

Through a gap in the crowd, Sakuta managed to catch a glimpse of a familiar face and a black bunny suit.

Just as he remembered it.

The day he'd first met Mai.

His heart skipped a beat.

"Can I see your ticket?"

"Er, uh, yes."

The lady prompted him, and he fished his ticket out.

She handed over a wristband—proof of admission.

"Show this to the man at the gate if you step out."

"Will do."

He was already on his way in.

He looked left and right and saw only crowds.

It was impossible to see more than a few yards in any direction.

He stretched up, looking for those ears.

She'd been going toward the smaller warehouse. He headed that way, hoping to glimpse the ears again—and finally caught sight of them twenty yards ahead.

"There!"

He tried to close the distance, but in this crowd, speed was not an option. When he tried to avoid the person moving in from the right, he almost hit the person on his left.

But the bunny ears seemed to have no problem moving forward, steadily getting farther and farther away.

Nobody seemed to notice her.

Even though practically everyone was here to see Mai Sakurajima.

And Mai was wandering around in a bunny costume…

No one noticed when the bunny girl vanished into the shadow of the brick building either.

Clearly, only Sakuta could see her.

He finally made it out of the crowd around the entrance and hurried around the building after her.

This was the crew parking lot. Because of the music festival, there were a bunch of tour buses in a row. A restricted area meant for the performers.

Naturally, there was an expandable fence set up to keep the crowds at bay. Five or six security guards were on the lookout.

The bunny girl waltzed right past them.

No one tried to stop her.

She moved with purpose, like she knew where she was headed.

Sakuta tried to follow, and a burly guard stopped him.

"Staff only, no entrance allowed."

The fence was only thigh high. He could just vault over it. But if he did that, the guards would tackle him. Not a promising prospect.

"I know people here…," he said, but he had no follow-through. The look it earned him was very dubious, and his eyes swam. But that wandering gaze found on a familiar face. "Oh, Hanawa!"

Mai's manager was on the phone some ten yards away—Ryouko Hanawa.

She jumped at her name, turned toward him, and looked surprised to see Sakuta standing there.

Wrapping up the call, she came over.

"What's this about?"

"Just need to talk to Mai real quick."

"About?"

"It's important!"

The bunny girl was still walking through the staff area. That beautiful pale back. The round tail above her hindquarters. Long, slim legs. Heels clicking as she went.

"Then use this."

Perhaps bowled over by the urgency in his tone, Ryouko pulled a staff badge out of her pocket. He hung it around his neck and vaulted over the fence.

"Where is she?"

"In the back, bus two."

She glanced toward the ten tour buses.

That was all he needed. Shouting a "Thank you!" over his shoulder, Sakuta raced off through the staff area.

He was back on the bunny girl's tail.

She vanished around the corner of the second bus.

The one Mai was in.

A moment later, Sakuta dived into the gap between the buses.

"Mai!"

He'd called his girlfriend's name any number of times before, but he yelled it again as he sprinted to the door.

"Mai!"

One more time as he climbed inside.

She answered quickly.

"Sakuta?"

She poked her head around a seat in the back, looking surprised and baffled.

"Anything happen?" he asked, rushing down the aisle, checking every seat for signs of the bunny girl.

He found none.

It was just Mai and Sakuta.

"Like what?" Mai asked, getting to her feet.

She was in full costume, but he was in no state to appreciate that.

"I saw bunny-girl Mai."

Just to be sure, he turned back, scanning the bus interior once more. He looked in the driver's seat to make sure no one was there. He checked the makeup stand. Even opened the fridge.

He'd inspected every seat (and under them as well) but found no one.

Only he and Mai were on this bus.

"I swear she came in here."

"I didn't see a thing. Ryouko went out to make a call, and then you came in."

"On the way from the station, I also saw red-knapsack Mai and white-dress Mai—you know, from the heart-condition movie. Not something I'd easily confuse."

He found it hard to chalk this up to his imagination.

But it was a fact that only the two of them were here.

"Mai, you're sure nothing's wrong?"

"Nothing at all."

"You're *sure* sure?"

"Are *you* okay, Sakuta?"

She moved slowly toward the driver's seat with a concerned expression.

"I'm fine."

"Really?"

When she asked again to make sure, he reconsidered.

He could see his face in Mai's eyes, and he looked rather upset. He could tell why Mai seemed worried. Maybe he was making her worry.

"Um, Mai…"

"What?"

"Feel free to say no, but can I get a hug?"

"Well, okay. Go on!"

Mai held her arms up, half-teasing.

Sakuta took her up on it, stepping forward and putting his arms around her slim shoulders and back.

"My stylist'll kill me if you wrinkle anything."

He stopped himself from squeezing her tight.

But they were still close enough for him to feel her heartbeat. Her warmth. Her breath on his ear. She leaned against him just enough for him to feel her weight.

"You like me here and now, better than little knapsack me."

"Absolutely."

"You like this me better than the old white-dress version."

"Naturally."

"You like hugging me like this better than that bunny girl."

"That's a tough call."

"If you can make jokes, then you're okay."

Mai pushed his chest, signaling the end of their embrace.

But Sakuta didn't let go.

He wasn't ready.

"The best Mai is you hugging me *in* a bunny-girl outfit."

"If that'll stop you from hallucinating, I might consider it."

"Weird. I was supposed to be the one worried about *you*."

How'd she turn the tables on me?

"Well, I guess I'm just gonna have to feast my eyes on this beautiful dress."

Deciding that he'd hung on long enough, Sakuta finally let her go.

"Do it," she said, flashing him an impish grin. Her stage costume *was* beautiful.

An announcement came over the loudspeakers outside.

"Attention all concertgoers. Sakuta Azusagawa from Fujisawa, your friend is waiting for you. Please come to the front entrance. I repeat—"

"They're calling you."

"That's so Akagi…"

2

He found Ikumi at reception, and they hit up the food stands as the skies darkened. The warehouses were bathed in orange lights. The music festival venue faced the water, and across that, they had a good view of the lights on the cruise ships anchored at Osanbashi Pier.

It was almost time for Mai's show, and the crowds steadily grew denser.

Half an hour before the scheduled start time, it was so packed they could barely see a few feet in any direction.

"Even more people than in the dream."

He couldn't tell exact numbers, but it felt like three times the size of the dream crowd.

The space before the main stage couldn't hold the crowd, and they were overflowing into the area meant for the second stage (on the opposite side of the square).

"Everyone saw those #dreaming posts. Not that I'm one to talk."

True—in Sakuta's dream, Ikumi hadn't been here.

The #dreaming posts were widely believed to predict the future, and that was enough to make people like Ikumi change their plans.

In the night sky, the stars of spring were twinkling—just like in his dream. Regulus in Leo. Spica in Virgo. Arcturus in Boötes.

Sakuta located each in turn while the main-stage lights were out.

As they came back on, the rock band started playing.

A roar, almost a shriek, went up from the crowd.

Four men driving the audience crazy were the band from Sakuta's dream. A guitar/vocalist. A bassist. A keyboardist. And a drummer.

"……The opening song."

"To what?"

"A TV show that just went off the air."

Ikumi knew more than he did.

They were standing shoulder to shoulder but had to yell to hear each other.

Mai was a guest vocalist and had yet to take the stage.

But the crowd was already hopping to the beat. Like ripples running through the whole venue, making them all move as one.

The crowd's excitement had reached a fever pitch—but the first song lasted less than four minutes.

When it ended, the venue felt impossibly quiet. Like the last few minutes had never happened.

In the silence, anticipation was building.

Everyone was waiting for Mai.

The vocalist picked up on that and shrugged.

He pulled the mic stand in close.

"It was *supposed* to be a surprise," he grumbled.

The crowd laughed.

"But oh well. Let's just have fun with it!"

He moved the stand to the side of the stage...and the drummer started the next song.

The one Mai sang in the movie, in character.

"I'm gonna keep on singing this song! Right here!"

Yelling a line from the movie, Mai ran onto the stage.

As she reached the center, she started belting out the lyrics.

The crowd's energy slammed into her like a shockwave.

Mai stood her ground onstage, singing hard enough to match the power of a crowd thirty thousand strong.

The temperature rose even higher, a pulsing vortex of emotion.

Unseen forces echoed through them, threatening to swallow them whole.

And Mai was at the heart of that overwhelming energy.

Her voice soared, and she pointed at the crowd. They went wild.

The crowd pulsed like the earth was rumbling, like they were trying to summon an eldritch monster from the depths of the ocean.

This number also lasted less than four minutes, but by the time it ended, it felt like half an hour had passed. The air in the venue was electric as a general sense of excitement and satisfaction swept through the audience.

The drummer hit the final cymbal crash.

The hush that followed had a murmur running through it. A low-level tension.

There was a brief lull, then the male singer said, "A big thank-you to our guest vocalist, Mai Sakurajima."

"Thank you!" Mai said, smiling and waving to the crowd. She bowed low.

The applause was thunderous.

Mai was only here for this one song.

All she had to do was straighten up, say a few more words, and walk offstage while waving.

That was the plan Sakuta had heard.

But before she could, a cry went up from the crowd.

"Encore!"

At first, it was one voice.

But soon...

"Encore!"

...several hundred joined in.

"Encore!"

The third call was a chorus, venue-wide.

"Encore! Encore!"

No one told them to.

"Encore! Encore!"

But thirty thousand people were all clapping together.

"Encore! Kirishima!"

And the chant began to change.

"Encore! Touko!"

The calls took on a mind of their own.

"Encore! Encore!"

No signs of it stopping.

"Touko Kirishima!"

The uncanny scene showed no sign of ending.

"Azusagawa," Ikumi said, shooting him an anxious look.

"This is the perfect chance to refute the charges."

If everyone wanted her to talk about it, that gave Mai a golden opportunity.

She had to see this as an opportunity.

Sakuta was sure of it.

But things quickly took a turn.

Before Mai's head came up, the drummer started tapping the high hat. The snare and bass drums soon joined in.

Then the bassist stated strumming.

The music made the encore cries fade out.

Anticipation. Rising expectations.

When the keyboard joined in, that switched to *certainty*.

Thirty thousand people oohed and aahed at once.

They knew that melody.

They knew this song…

…and whose song it was.

Even Sakuta did.

"That's Touko Kirishima's…," Ikumi muttered, eyes glued to the stage.

Then they saw Mai's head come up.

A smile was on her lips.

She took a deep breath and held the mic to her lips.

Her voice soared over the crowd.

I'm glad I met you.

Just like he'd dreamed it.

The song from the dream.

That's not how I see things.

My soulmate's no longer out there.

* * *

The crowd was stunned, focused purely on Mai.

This was why they'd come here, but it still hit hard.

But the love songs we listened to all agree.
We will meet again.

Sakuta was frozen to the spot.

Her voice rose.

Soaring.

A strong, beautiful voice that matched the band's performance note for note.

Don't be afraid to get lost.
Get up, fling that door open, step outside.

What was he seeing?

What was he being shown?

Sakuta's mind filled with questions.

He knew the girl holding the mic.

Everyone in Japan knew her.

She was Mai Sakurajima, former child star, still acting in movies and TV shows.

She was definitely *Mai*.

But the future's not guaranteed.
I'll be alone again tomorrow.
No one to split things with.
This empty hollow in my heart.

* * *

Mai sang the exact same way she did in the dream.

Like this was her song.

Like she was Touko Kirishima.

The crowd was speechless. They didn't sway to the rhythm, didn't clap along. Everyone just stood there, stunned.

If I have to feel like this…
I wish I'd never met you.

As the crowd's surprise began to fade, Mai finished the Touko Kirishima song. It was a surprisingly short song that didn't even last two minutes. The band's performance faded out.

The coastal venue became as quiet as any ordinary day. A hush settled over the crowd. Yet in the darkness, thirty thousand people stood.

They were holding their breath and waiting for Mai to speak.

Their impatience was palpable. Any second now.

Onstage, Mai must have felt their expectations. And for that reason, she offered a sheepish smile.

She took a breath.

Sakuta recognized each movement.

It was just like the dream.

Mai raised the mic to her mouth again.

"I'd like to take this moment to share something with you all."

The crowd stayed still. They were watching her every move.

"I imagine some of you have already figured it out."

Mai paused again, scanning the crowd.

Every mind here was champing at the bit. Mai shut her eyes, soaking it in. When her eyes opened once more…

…she said, "I'm Touko Kirishima."

A full second of silence followed.

Then another.

Then all that built-up anticipation erupted. Without anything to hold it back, time began moving once again. A roar shook the air like a thunderclap. The mood had completely changed.

Nothing but cheers filled the venue.

"Azusagawa, what does this mean?"

Only Sakuta and Ikumi were left reeling.

"How should I know?"

He'd meant that as an answer but had no idea if she'd heard. The roar of the crowd swallowed their words.

Surrounded by cheering people, they stood perfectly still, unable to move.

Their eyes were still on the stage—on Mai.

She'd called herself Touko Kirishima. She felt so far away. Until the concert ended, Sakuta stood rooted to the spot, muttering "Why? What for?" to himself on a loop.

3

Mai's turn ended and the stage emptied, yet most of the crowd stuck around. They were basking in the afterglow, and no one was ready to leave.

The tension in the air felt hot and heavy. It imparted an odd sense of unity to the audience.

Sakuta threaded his way through that crowd to the staff area. He lost Ikumi somewhere along the way, but he put seeing Mai first.

He showed the guards his pass and was allowed in.

He headed back to the second bus, Mai's greenroom.

As he stepped inside, he blurted, "Mai, what was that?"

He was trying to keep his cool but couldn't stop himself.

"Is that any way to greet a girlfriend after a show? Try 'Great concert; you were amazing.'"

Mai was by the vanity, taking off her earrings. There was a cheery note in her voice, as if she was relieved it had gone well. Like the crowd, she was still carrying the rush of the concert with her.

The exact opposite of the desperation Sakuta brought in.

"It was a great show. Just…"

"Just…?" Mai repeated, eyes on the mirror as she took off the other earring.

"Why'd you lie?"

"What lie?" she asked, not changing her tone at all.

"About you being Touko Kirishima."

In the mirror, their eyes met.

She glanced away, taking off the costume's necklace and rings. Each piece went into their dedicated cases on the vanity. For the finishing touch, she took a heart-shaped ring out of another case. The ring he'd given her for her birthday. Only when it was on the ring finger of her right hand did she turn to face Sakuta.

"I feel bad for keeping it from you, Sakuta. But agency orders. I didn't tell Nodoka, either."

"That's not what I'm asking."

"I don't blame you for balking. I've told you to your face I'm not Touko Kirishima."

"Then you really are…?"

He couldn't finish. Something made him hesitate.

"I am Touko Kirishima."

Mai said the words he'd been reluctant to say out loud.

Too easily.

She made it seem as if it was the most natural thing in the world.

Like it was a simple statement of fact.

She had looked Sakuta right in the eye and said something he knew was wrong.

When he didn't budge, she said it again, gently. "I am Touko Kirishima."

She'd denied it just yesterday.

She'd given no indication of it minutes before the concert.

Sakuta's heart showed not one sign of being swayed by this. Not one flicker of doubt.

He was drowning in a sea of confusion.

"No chance this is an April Fool's joke?"

"If I'm lying here, I must be a great actress," she said with a laugh, smiling.

"Mai, you *are* a great actress."

He didn't feel like smiling back.

At the least, it didn't seem like she was deceiving him.

Mai genuinely believed she was Touko Kirishima.

She had that unnatural naturalness to her.

"Done changing, Mai?" Ryouko poked her head in the door and found Mai still in costume. "Better get out of that, or we'll miss the Shinkansen."

"Mai, you've got plans?"

"Filming in Kobe tomorrow morning. We have to get there tonight."

"Which is why it's time for you to head outside, Sakuta," Ryouko said, waving to the door.

"We'll talk more when I'm back from the shoot," Mai said.

He couldn't exactly linger. And talking more right now would not fish him out of this whirlpool.

"Just one more thing, Mai."

"What?"

"I love you."

Mai's smile was somewhat bashful. Her expressions and gestures were every bit the Mai he knew and loved.

"Sakuta."

"What?"

"I love you, too."

She flashed an impish grin. That, too, was *his* Mai.

Outside the bus, it felt instantly darker.

He could swear he was melting into the darkness, his shoes and the asphalt fusing together.

Mindful of the fuzzy boundaries, he tried walking and soon found someone waiting for him outside the staff area.

Ikumi.

Her head was down, lit from below by the screen of her phone.

Sakuta stepped over the fence and approached, calling, "You didn't have to wait."

"I'm invested."

"Yeah, I figured."

"So?"

"Is this what getting bamboozled feels like? Mai seems to genuinely think she is Touko Kirishima."

"Like Nene Iwamizawa and the other Santas?"

"Not sure. Feels different. It's still definitely Mai, and she doesn't have a reason to become Touko Kirishima like they did."

"True."

"And everyone could see her."

That point alone was fundamentally different from Nene and the Santa Squad.

"Footage of the concert's spreading on social media. Everyone thinks Sakurajima really is Touko Kirishima."

Ikumi glanced back down at her phone.

"Mai did become invisible back in high school."

"I heard something like that from the other me. The whole school was acting like she wasn't there, and eventually, no one could perceive her at all."

"I wonder if something similar is going on here," Sakuta said.

Ikumi soon caught his gist.

"Everyone believed Touko Kirishima was actually Sakurajima, so that came true?"

Sakuta nodded glumly.

"Maybe that explains the red-knapsack Sakurajima you saw."

"Does it?"

"You saw the Mai Sakurajima the crowd around you was picturing."

That did make sense.

"Maybe I did."

But this wasn't the time to dig into it.

"In high school, you asked her out in front of the whole school, and that fixed things?"

"Yeah, I rewrote the students' perceptions."

"If you tried the same thing here…"

"I might well be forced to propose with the whole world watching."

Minegahara High had roughly a thousand students.

But far more people believed Mai Sakurajima and Touko Kirishima were one and the same. With the news already spreading online, that number was likely in the millions. And that might be lowballing it.

"Azusagawa, you don't think you can alter everyone's perceptions at once, do you?"

"......"

He couldn't say he could.

And didn't want to say he couldn't.

If Mai was involved, he had to.

But his long silence proved all the answer Ikumi needed.

"Sorry, that's unanswerable."

"If it is possible, there's only one way."

"Namely...?"

"Gotta get the *real* Touko Kirishima to step forward."

"Then you'll have to look for her."

When she said that, Sakuta felt a pin drop.

"......Maybe that's what it meant."

"Huh?"

"'Mai's in danger.'"

Ikumi's eyes went wide. It was clear she felt the same. A moment later, she let out a voiceless yelp.

Like someone had just put their hands on her.

"What?"

"......"

In lieu of an answer, she looked down at her left palm.

"Message from the other world?" he asked.

"Azusagawa, it's for you," Ikumi said, holding up her hand.

There was familiar handwriting in black pen.

Two short lines.

―――*Stop Touko Kirishima.*
―――*Before reality is rewritten.*
It was Sakuta's handwriting.
But this didn't make sense.
"What does it mean?" he asked, looking up.
"Don't ask me," she said as she pulled a black pen out of her purse. "Ask him."
"You came prepared."
"I simply carried it around in case this happened."
"That's what I meant."
He took the pen and popped the cap off.
"Write away," she said, holding out the hand with nothing on it.
―――*What do you mean by rewrite reality?*
Sakuta started writing.
The answer appeared one letter at a time, on Ikumi's left palm.
―――*I wasn't able to observe Touko Kirishima.*
This raised even more questions.
Before Sakuta could ask any of those, more letters appeared.
―――*My perceptions may be revised soon.*
The writing was going up Ikumi's wrist now.
―――*The rest is in your hands,*
Unable to peel his eyes away, he watched the writing move up her arm.
―――*phoneless Adoles*
The message broke off midword.
―――*Adolescent what?*
Sakuta wrote out his question, but no answer came.
Instead…
"Sorry," Ikumi muttered. "Feels like the connection's gone."

She looked downcast.

"Okay," he said, pulling the pen away from her skin and putting the lid back on. "Right."

All he could do was stand there and nod.

4

The train was running through a residential area. Warm lights streamed past outside the windows, proof of life.

Sakuta stood by the door, oblivious to all of that. His eyes were moving with the scenery, but his mind was elsewhere.

He'd parted ways with Ikumi at Yokohama Station and boarded the Tokaido Line. It was just crowded enough to fill the seats. Most passengers had their eyes on their phones or seemed to be sleeping.

The sights inside the train weren't changing.

Sakuta himself stood still while his mind kept running over the events of the day again and again.

Things had been normal when he'd woken up.

Nasuno stepping on his face, breakfast with the cat, making more food once Kaede finally got up…

She'd been half-asleep even as she ate but woke up enough to leave just after noon—off to see her old friend Kotomi Kano. They'd planned to attend a Sweet Bullet concert.

Sakuta had seen her out, then got ready to leave himself and was out the door by two PM.

He'd taken a train from Fujisawa to Yokohama Station, then switched to the Minatomirai Line and met Ikumi on the platform.

Up until that point, there was nothing out of the ordinary.

Things only got weird at Bashamichi Station.

He's spotted little Mai in that brick building. With her red knapsack. And not just once—the second time, Mai was a tween.

Outside the station, he'd seen her in a white dress, the one Mai'd worn in the movie where her character had a heart condition.

And at the music festival venue, he'd seen Mai dressed as a bunny girl.

He didn't think he'd been seeing things.

He'd met Mai on the tour bus before the concert and sensed nothing amiss.

She'd been acting normal.

He was the one who hadn't been acting normal, and she'd been worried about him.

When she'd hugged him, it had felt like it always did.

Every bit as soft and warm an embrace as any other day.

He'd concluded he didn't have to worry.

But the result…

She'd gotten up onstage to stake a wild claim.

——*"I'm Touko Kirishima."*

Just remembering it was unsettling.

It didn't feel real.

Like he was dreaming right now.

He certainly hoped he was.

The way Mai had acted after the show only made things worse.

She'd been herself—other than insisting she really was Touko Kirishima.

What she'd said was ununsual, but how she'd acted wasn't.

And that itself seemed strange.

The finishing blow had been the message Ikumi received from the other potential world.

──*Stop Touko Kirishima.*
──*Before reality is rewritten.*
What had the other Sakuta been trying to say? He couldn't grasp much of it. Their conversation had cut out too soon.

Several things he'd said were concerning.

It sure felt like things were going very wrong.

And Touko Kirishima was at the heart of it.

But was it even possible for him to do something? When the other Sakuta hadn't been able to perceive her at all?

In his second year of high school, he'd paid a visit to that other world and gained a distinct impression that that world's Sakuta was better at everything.

He was still thinking about these things when the train dropped him off in Fujisawa.

He kept thinking about them on the walk from the station.

Looping back and forth through the day.

But all this thinking didn't get him anywhere. The only place he managed to get to was the door of his apartment building.

"Guess I should call Futaba."

He hopped off the elevator and went to his apartment door. After taking a moment to fish the key out of his pocket, Sakuta unlocked it.

"I'm home, Nasuno," he called, and the cat meowed, poking her head out of the living room.

A moment later...

"Oh! Sakuta, welcome home!"

A tall, thin, black-and-white creature.

Kaede, in panda pajamas.

Sakuta froze with his shoes half off.

"What are you doing, Kaede?"

"Welcoming you home!"

He could see that. She was super enthusiastic about it.

But that wasn't very Kaede at all. His frown deepened.

"……"

Sakuta studied her face.

Something seemed odd.

"Sakuta?"

Kaede leaned diagonally, studying his scowl.

He knew that body language.

He knew the look on her face.

This was his *other* sister, the one who always wore panda pajamas.

His rational mind was screaming that this couldn't be possible.

But once the thought struck him, he couldn't dismiss it.

The possibility reared up and escaped his lips.

"Is that you, *Kaede*?" he asked, putting a particular emphasis on her name.

"That's my name!"

She leaned even farther over, trying to figure out why he asked.

"Are you really?"

"Who else would I be, Sakuta?!"

Her tone was bright and cheery. She was a bit taller than he remembered, but he'd recognize that smile anywhere. This was, without a doubt, the Kaede who wrote her name in hiragana.

Seeing that expression sent ripples through him.

Once more, he felt like he must be dreaming.

That was partially due to his sheer surprise, but that wasn't the main emotion.

His brain hadn't caught up enough to be happy.

His feelings were still in turmoil.

He couldn't quite process this.

As he wandered through the woods, unable to find a way out…

"*The bath is full,*" an electronic voice said.

"Do you wanna go first?" she asked.

"Nah…"

That was less an answer than a by-product of his confusion.

"Then I'll take the first round!" Kaede declared, not at all bothered by his behavior.

She padded away into the living room, then came hustling back with a change of clothes and entered the washroom.

Sakuta stared at the closed door, stunned.

After a while, he heard water running.

And then the phone rang, calling to him from the living room. On pure reflex, he finished taking his shoes off and stepped into the apartment. His feet took him down the hall.

The lights on the phone were flashing. He picked up the receiver and held it to his ear.

"Yeah?" he said, his mind blank.

"Oh, Sakuta?" It was a very familiar voice.

He recognized the number on the display.

This was the original Kaede's voice. Her number.

"……"

He stopped thinking completely.

"Um, Sakuta? Are you there?"

He heard her voice on the line again, and he said "Yeah" automatically.

What was this?

What was happening?

"Kaede?"

"Why was that a question?" she laughed, like he was half-asleep.

"Are you really Kaede?"

"Obviously. What's the matter?"

That was unmistakably her voice.

"Anyway, I'm gonna stay at Mom and Dad's place tonight. Forgot to mention it on the way out but figured you'd want a heads-up."

That attitude and tone made it clear which Kaede he was talking to on the phone.

But then what was the other Kaede doing *here*? Waiting for him to get home?

One Kaede in the bath, the other on the phone with him.

Both existed at the same time.

That should've been impossible.

"Oh, right! Sweet Bullet news! They announced it at the end of the show today! They're going to Budokan! I've gotta be there! ……Earth to Sakuta?"

"I hear you."

Those words came out reflexively.

He had heard her loud and clear.

He was listening.

But his brain wasn't processing any of it. It had ground to a halt.

"Uh, Kaede…"

"What?"

"Can you stay with Mom and Dad for a while?"

"Well, I was already planning on staying through spring break. Why?"

"No reason."

He had no clue what else to say.

He sure as hell couldn't tell her about the other Kaede.

Chapter 2
Walking Through the Fog

1

The next morning began with Nasuno's feet on his face. Even with his eyes screwed shut, Sakuta could feel those paws counting one, two, one, two.

He was forced to open his eyes halfway, blearily looking up at his cat.

"Morning, Nasuno," he said through a yawn.

His lids soon lost the battle against sleep and closed again.

It felt like he had woken up on the wrong side of the bed.

Sakuta knew why he was out of sorts. He had been tossing and turning all night.

For so many reasons…

So much had happened the day before. Too much.

Hiragana Kaede meeting him at the door had really hit hard. If his heart was stormier than the sea. He didn't find it easy to drift off in that condition, much less get any rest once he did.

He'd slept fitfully, constantly waking himself back up. When he finally did sleep for real, it was getting light out behind the curtains. That was only an hour or two ago.

Another big yawn.

He would've loved to just roll back over.

But he made himself check the clock instead.

Seven thirty-two AM.

Sunday, April 2.

In other words, the day after April Fool's. The day after the music festival in Yokohama's Red Brick Warehouse.

"So much for a twist ending where that was all a dream…"

And as if punishing him for that false hope…

"Nasuno, is he up?"

A voice from the hall.

The other Kaede's voice.

Nasuno meowed back and slipped past the door. Sakuta hauled himself out of bed and yawned a third time as he followed the cat into the hall.

In the living room, he found Kaede smiling in panda pajamas.

"Oh, Sakuta! Good morning! Breakfast is all ready!"

She waved to the table, where toast, scrambled eggs, sausage, and cherry tomatoes awaited. A common morning meal in their house.

"You made all that?"

"These eggs are Mai's secret recipe!"

"They are?"

"I'm now a licensed professional."

She puffed herself up with pride. Her confidence was not unfounded—the eggs looked very good. Exactly like the ones Mai sometimes made.

"Then let's see what professional cooking tastes like."

"Great!" Kaede cried.

He sat down across from her. This Kaede was sitting where the original Kaede usually sat these days. She'd scooped eggs onto the toast and was happily munching away, looking like a portrait of happiness.

And that only made Sakuta feel like he was lost in an uncanny forest.

This was definitely hiragana Kaede.

There was no doubt about that.

"……"

It still didn't feel real. More like he was actively dreaming.

"You're not eating, Sakuta!"

"I am," he said, following her lead and scooping scrambled eggs onto his toast.

The crunch of the toast complemented the fluffy eggs perfectly, filling his mouth with joy.

"That's good," he said.

"I'm licensed." She beamed again.

"So, Kaede…"

"What?"

"How long have we been here?"

"Four whole years! We'll start year five before April ends!"

"Thought so."

"Sakuta, you are very out of it this morning," she said, eyes gleaming like a detective on the case.

"You caught me."

"In which case I have no choice but to make you some coffee."

Kaede hopped up and moved to the kitchen.

From behind, it was clear she'd grown since he last saw her. Sakuta and hiragana Kaede had moved to this Fujisawa apartment four years ago. The spring he started high school. She'd regained her memories and reverted to the original Kaede again in the fall of his second year.

He only knew the other Kaede when she was in junior high.

The face peeping out of those panda pajamas wasn't quite as childish.

The math checked out for the timeline she'd given.

She'd lived here four years.

Almost five.

And she'd been hiragana Kaede that whole time.

"Okay, Sakuta. Here you go!"

She came back from the kitchen and put a steaming mug in front of him. It had a tanuki on it.

"Thanks."

He took a sip. A tad bitter. But that told him this was real. Not a dream, not his imagination, but real life.

He would have to work through things one at a time. Figure out what was real before yesterday, and what was real now.

"What'd you do yesterday, Kaede?"

"At lunch, I went to school and got materials ready to welcome new students to the club."

"School?"

"Minegahara High?" she said like it was obvious, crooking her head at him.

"Club?"

"The Animal Club?" The doubt in her eyes was growing stronger.

"Right, I knew that."

Clearly, this Kaede had made it into Minegahara. And joined something called the Animal Club.

"If we don't get some new members, the future of our club is in trouble!"

"Well, you'd better work hard recruiting them."

"That's the plan!"

She clenched both fists, demonstrating motivation.

"Yesterday was a big surprise," she said, changing topics.

"Mm?"

"Mai was Touko Kirishima all along?!"

He had not expected her to bring that up like she was making small talk. Her sunny tone was just what Sakuta expected from her. She clearly didn't doubt the news at all.

"You saw the concert?"

"I watched a stream!"

She glanced at the coffee table. There was a laptop on it. She must have watched it there.

"Do you think Mai really is Touko Kirishima?" Sakuta asked.

"......What do you mean?" She leaned way over, her confusion manifesting physically. "Mai said she was. Didn't she?"

"......I guess she did."

"......?"

The confusion was not fading away. Before it could, there was a beep from the washroom.

"The laundry machine's calling!"

Shoving the last of her toast in her mouth, Kaede hopped up and ran off like it was second nature. She'd evidently learned a lot more housework than he remembered. She'd grown quite a bit over these four years.

That put a smile on his face, but it wasn't completely worry-free. He still had no clue what he was supposed to make of this.

Too many questions about the facts before him.

He wasn't even sure this was real.

It felt like he'd gotten lost in the fog yesterday and hadn't found his way out yet.

He needed to get a handle on things.

He gulped down the last of his scrambled eggs, got up, reached for the landline, and punched in an eleven-digit number from memory.

The first person he wanted to call was Rio Futaba, a friend from high school.

It rang twice, then she picked up.

"It's me, Futaba. Sorry for calling this early. You got a minute?"

He was trying to maintain his cool, but he couldn't stop himself rushing through the words.

"Futaba is not able to come to the phone right now."

Sakuta had not expected a man's voice.

"Leave your message after the beep," the voice joked.

Sakuta recognized it right away. Another high school friend—Yuuma Kunimi.

"Why are you picking up?"

"Huh? Well, I figured it'd be fine to answer your call."

He wasn't sure what that meant.

"And Futaba?"

"She's in the hot spring."

Even more unexpected.

"Huh?" he said. A very dumb noise.

"She's in the hot spring," Yuuma repeated, like it was nothing.

"Why a hot spring?"

"Well, after you regaled us with tales of your hot springs date with Sakurajima, we wanted to see what all the fuss is about," he said in a joking tone.

"So you're staying the night?"

"Well, yeah."

"Kunimi, I never took you for the cheating type."

Sakuta meant to call out his friend, but he mostly sounded surprised.

"Cheating how?" Yuuma cackled. There was no trace of guilt in his voice.

It was at this point that Sakuta started to realize something was wrong.

Their discussion wasn't making any sense.

"What about Kamisato?"

Yuuma could hardly ignore that name.

"What about her? We broke up two years ago. You know that."

"Huh?"

Another dumb noise.

"You okay there, Sakuta? You're acting weird."

Yuuma was laughing like he was talking to an old friend. Enjoying the banter.

"Hang on, Kunimi. You mean you and Futaba are dating?"

"A bit late for that!"

Sakuta felt his pulse quickening.

"You're really dating?"

Unease left his lips quivering.

"We sure are."

The inside of his mouth felt dry.

"Since when?" he managed to croak.

"Since fall of last year, when I got back from training. That enough for you?"

"……"

He didn't manage to say it was.

His head was spinning.

Yuuma's words had put him in a tailspin.

"Oh, and so it *was* Sakurajima all along! The real Touko Kirishima."

While Sakuta was still reeling from the revelation that they were dating, Yuuma casually dropped that topic in their conversation. That saved Sakuta the trouble of having to ask it himself, but he hadn't managed to calm down enough to tackle this new subject yet.

He took a few short, shallow breaths.

"……You believe that, Kunimi?" he managed to ask.

"I haven't seen the vid, but she announced it at the festival, right? I just checked my feed, and everyone was talking about it."

"Did Futaba say anything?"

He could feel his hand tightening around the phone. The tension rising up from his feet had made him grip it much harder than he'd intended.

"Mm? Uh, she said, 'Poor Azusagawa, he'll see even less of her.'"

He was ultra-focused on his ears, not wanting to miss a syllable.

"I imagine Sakurajima will be even busier now."

But this was the last thing he wanted to hear. Definitely not good.

"……So even Futaba bought the announcement."

Apparently, she also believed Touko Kirishima was Mai Sakurajima.

…Despite specifically discussing how impossible that was with him.

"Oh, Futaba's out! Passing you along."

He could hear in the background, "It's Sakuta." "Why?" "Not sure." After that brief, breezy back-and-forth…

"What?" Rio's voice.

But at this point he wasn't sure what he should ask her about.

Mai claiming to be Touko Kirishima?

The message from the other potential world received via Ikumi's hand?

The Kaede waiting for him at home?

The original Kaede who called from their parents' house?

The fact that Yuuma and Rio were dating now?

There were too many strange occurrences.

Sakuta's brain couldn't sort through them at all.

He'd been hoping to talk to the Rio who wasn't dating Yuuma and who knew Mai wasn't Touko Kirishima.

But the Rio on the phone was dating Yuuma and thought Mai was Touko Kirishima. What should he talk to this Rio about? Where should he begin?

"Azusagawa?" she asked, when he said nothing.

"So, Futaba…"

"So, what?"

"The Futaba I know isn't dating Kunimi."

"……"

"What kind of Adolescence Syndrome is that?"

He'd ultimately gone with the most direct option.

"You're *still* talking about Adolescence Syndrome, Azusagawa? You turn twenty next week."

"True."

The calendar in the living room had a big circle in red around April 10, with *Sakuta's Birthday!* in hiragana Kaede's handwriting.

"But the Futaba I know really—"

He tried to stick to his guns, but she cut him off.

"You don't want me dating Kunimi?" she asked gravely.

"I'm all for it. Obviously."

"Well, good."

It didn't sound like she was convinced.

"I've hoped you two would get together since high school."

Sakuta absolutely meant that.

But even then, he'd been perfectly aware that would never happen. Yuuma was in love with someone else. Or should have been…

"Okay…"

This time she sounded more convinced, or possibly relieved.

"Tell me, Futaba…"

"What?"

"Are you happy?"

"……"

She inhaled like he'd caught her off guard.

There was a brief silence.

It was easy to picture how she filled it. Yuuma was in the room with her; she must have glanced at him. He'd have noticed and smiled purely because Rio was looking at him.

It was practically a foregone conclusion when she said, "Of course I'm happy," sounding bashful.

Sakuta could hardly insist this must be some mistake.

Even if he did, there was no way she would accept that.

At best, she'd conclude he was talking crazy and become worried about him.

It would not lead to the future he was hoping for.

"Is that all, Azusagawa?" she asked, dubious.

"Not quite."

"What else?"

"Be happy together."

"Mm. Want him back on?"

"Nah, I'm good. Sorry I bothered you."

With that, he hung up.

"……"

Sakuta put the receiver back in the cradle and stood there. His hand was still on it. He hadn't moved at all.

Honestly, he understood even less now than before he'd made the call. It had only added to his problems.

But the call with Rio had felt familiar somehow.

"Come to think of it, Futaba had said she'd dreamed she was out with Kunimi…"

She'd said it felt like they were together.

That was part of the inexplicable Christmas incident, where so many young people posted about their prophetic dreams that it brought the servers down. The story got picked up by the news and morning shows and was still a hot topic through the New Year's holiday.

On Christmas morning, Kaede had mentioned she'd dreamed about reverting to the other one.

Sakuta's dream had been about Mai claiming she was Touko Kirishima.

Three dreams had come true.

"Is that what rewriting reality means?"

"What's happening now?" Kaede asked, coming out of the washroom. She'd heard him talking to himself.

"Wish I knew."

If the message from the other potential world was right, the cause lay with Touko Kirishima.

——*Stop Touko Kirishima.*

He'd read those words, but yesterday, he'd been unsure why that was necessary.

Now, though, he was starting to feel like he had to act fast.

The other Sakuta had characterized this as rewriting reality, but to Sakuta's mind, it was even worse.

The world he thought he knew was collapsing.

Fears smoldered in the pit of his stomach.

His pulse raced.

He felt desperate to escape this predicament.

"Sakuta, you've got a restaurant shift starting at lunchtime?"

"Maybe I do."

He sounded out of it.

"Then we'd better give Nasuno her bath this morning."

"Good point…"

He started to respond the same way, but halfway through, an idea struck him.

"Ack, sorry, Kaede. Got something to take care of before work."

"Very well. I'll give Nasuno her bath all by myself!"

Nasuno meowed at her feet.

There was something Sakuta had to confirm with his own two eyes.

He wanted visual confirmation that both Kaedes really did exist at once.

2

He left the house just past nine AM.

"Have fun, Sakuta!" Kaede yelled, carrying Nasuno into the bathroom.

Outside the building, he was greeted by a blue sky.

Clear spring air and not a cloud in sight.

The polar opposite of his overcast heart, which made that blue look positively fake.

He stared up above for so long he got dizzy and had to bring his gaze back down to earth to collect himself.

At that precise moment—

"Yoo-hoo!"

That voice was too cheery for the hour.

He turned to the building across the street and saw someone waving at him.

It was the leader of the Sweet Bullet idol group, Uzuki Hirokawa. She'd been enrolled at his university but dropped out halfway through the year.

She came running over. "You good? I'm good!" she said, beaming as bright as the spring sun.

Nodoka was lurking behind her.

"I'm, uh, getting by."

"Oh! Sakuta, it's finally happening!"

"Kokugikan? Kaede told me."

"Noooo! It's the Budokan!"

"I could swear you said that was still a long way off."

Six months back, she'd definitely said as much. So had Nodoka.

"We worked really hard, and our fans cheered us on! Didn't you?"

"I can't wait to see you on that stage, Zukki."

He meant that.

"Woot!"

Uzuki threw both hands up, demanding a double high five.

"Either way, congrats."

"Thanks!" she said, as revved up as when she was onstage.

"Same to you, Toyohama. All good news," he said, glancing over Uzuki's shoulder.

"Yeah, well...," Nodoka said, rather subdued.

He'd have thought she'd be happier.

"You seem disgruntled."

"Nodoka's just sulking," Uzuki whispered. "Mai's announcement sucked all the hype out of our big news!"

"That's not true!" Nodoka snapped, hearing every word of that.

"Then what is it?"

"We live together, yet I had no idea? How oblivious am I?"

"You too, Toyohama?"

"Me too, what?"

"You think Mai's Touko Kirishima."

"Huh? She said so herself yesterday. Onstage."

"I saw the stream! What a show!" Uzuki said, leaning in enthusiastically.

"But Mai herself denied it repeatedly," Sakuta insisted.

"That's because of the contracts, obviously. Agency…record company…," Nodoka grumbled, not meeting his eyes.

"The commercial I did had a contract like that! I couldn't tell anyone until they ran the version that showed my face."

"……Yeah, that's what Mai said, too."

It was a logical explanation. The industry was full of those deals.

But Sakuta still found it hard to swallow. And it bugged him that Nodoka, Uzuki, and everyone else was so easily convinced. The nagging feeling that something was very wrong had taken up residence inside him. An unpleasant feeling that was only getting worse over time.

"What, you don't believe her, Sakuta?" Nodoka asked, seeing the look on his face.

"I dunno. It just doesn't sit right."

"What do you mean?!" Uzuki said, genuinely puzzled. If this had been a manga, there'd have been a question mark floating over her head.

"You were at the festival, right?" Nodoka asked. "Did you not talk to her in person?"

"I did."

"Huh? So what are you on about?"

When she asked, Nodoka looked baffled. As time went on, that shifted to anxiety and concern. All those emotions were directed at Sakuta.

For a moment, Uzuki glanced from one to the other, but soon she settled on giving him a worried look. She was obviously wondering if something was wrong.

"Are you okay, Sakuta?" she asked aloud.

Clearly, they suspected he wasn't.

They felt really far away.

They were right in front of him, but it didn't feel like it.

Close enough to touch...

But it seemed like if he reached out, they'd move that much further away.

Each word he used to close that gap pushed them away.

To escape that sensation, he changed the subject.

"Gonna miss my train."

"Ack, we've got a rehearsal to get to! Nodoka, let's book it!"

"If we miss the Romancecar, it's all your fault, Sakuta!"

All three started walking fast.

They pumped their legs one after the other, setting a high pace.

Each step carried them closer to the station—even though Sakuta felt unsteady on his feet. His brain and body seemed like they were out of sync. It was almost as if he'd forgotten how he usually walked. The more conscious of that he was, the worse it got.

Uzuki and Nodoka pulled ahead, and the whole way to the station, Sakuta thought of nothing but how walking worked...all the while wondering if any of this was real.

3

They'd jogged part of the way, and that proved enough for Nodoka and Uzuki to board the Romancecar to Shinjuku.

Sakuta saw them off through the Odakyu gates, then went up the stairs to the JR area. He tapped his IC commuter pass, stepped through the gates, and boarded an incoming Tokaido Line train.

Sakuta got off that train twenty minutes later, at Yokohama Station.

Ten AM, and the department store had just opened. Sakuta stopped in to buy some pudding. The kind that came in beakers with a hard-boiled detective featured on them.

The through-service train to Hachioji showed up just as he got back, so he boarded that.

One Kaede was back at the apartment, and one Kaede was staying with their parents.

To confirm that fact, Sakuta rode through Higashi-Kanagawa, Oguchi, Kikuna, and Shin-Yokohama and finally got off at Kozukue Station.

Outside the station, he followed the main road for a while, then turned onto a side street after around ten minutes. Already in sight of the company housing his parents lived in.

He took the stairs to the third floor, moved to the end of the row, and rang the intercom.

Three full seconds of silence.

"Yes?" That was his mother's voice over the speaker.

"It's me. Sakuta."

"Oh, what brings you here? Give me just a moment!"

The intercom cut out, and he heard footsteps coming.

The door opened.

"You lose your key?" Kaede asked.

Definitely the original Kaede. Same hair, tone of voice, attitude—no mistaking her.

"Sakuta?"

When he didn't answer, she shot him a frown, head crooked a bit.

"Left it at home," he said, and he grabbed the door and slipped inside. "I brought gifts."

He handed the box of pudding to Kaede and took his shoes off.

"Nice. Mom, he brought pudding!"

She happily showed the box to their mother, who'd also come to the entryway.

"Then that's our three o'clock snack."

"Aww, let's eat them now."

As they chattered, Sakuta stepped into the apartment.

"What brings you here?" his dad asked, looking up from his tablet—he was reading the newspaper. "Something going on?"

"Nah, once college starts, I won't have much time, so I figured I should stop by before spring break ends."

"Ah."

His father nodded vaguely and looked back at the tablet.

"You staying for lunch?"

"Oh, can't, got plans after this."

The other Kaede had claimed he had a lunchtime shift at the restaurant.

"What, a date with Mai?" his mother teased.

"Something like that."

He figured it best to go with her version. He was only here to confirm the original Kaede still existed with his own two eyes…and he wasn't about to tell anyone that. They probably wouldn't get it even if he did try to explain.

"Oh, right, Sakuta…," Kaede said.

"Mm?"

"Can we swap shifts next week?"

Oblivious to his predicament, she was business as usual.

"Is there a Sweet Bullet show?"

"I'm going to the hot springs in Hakone with Mom and Dad."

She glanced at the laptop on the table. It was open to the hot springs' homepage.

"I'm not invited?"

"You already went with Mai over Christmas."

"No rule against going twice."

"Just take my shift."

"Fine."

There was nothing remarkable about that exchange; that's how siblings always talked. How he and Kaede always talked.

And for some reason, that felt a bit odd.

He'd just chatted with the other Kaede this morning. They'd had breakfast and done the dishes, and she'd waved him out the door.

His internal alarm was going off.

They shouldn't *both* exist.

And yet they both seemed real.

A weird place to be, and he could not find a convincing explanation.

Just being around Kaede was rattling him.

"……Sakuta? Is there something on my face?"

He must have zonked out. She was scowling at him.

"Nope. Enjoy the hot springs."

"That's it?"

"Bring me back something."

That was the best he could manage now.

4

Sakuta stayed for a single cup of tea, then took his leave and headed back the way he'd come to Fujisawa.

He made it to the restaurant he worked at five minutes before his shift started, did a quick change, and punched his card with only a minute to spare.

Without batting an eye, he sailed out onto the floor, greeting a customer as they stepped in the door. He seated them, took their order, brought their food, cleared their dishes, rang them up, and bused the table. And did the same for each new arrival.

Rinse and repeat until the lunch rush died down, and the vibe shifted to a relaxed teatime.

With fewer orders coming in, he decided to resupply the drink bar.

"Azusagawa, take your break," his manager said as he grabbed the emptied boxes.

"Will do."

Sakuta piled those up out back, then headed for the staff break room.

No one else was there, so he flopped himself down on a folding chair. Someone had left a box of candy on the table—a souvenir—so he reached for that, and someone came in the door.

"Ugh, Senpai."

Tomoe Koga flinched at the sight of him.

She had a big parcel with her and tried to hide it, but she was petite and couldn't hide much. It was a flat bag, like a manta ray, the ends jutting out on either side of her. It looked like the kind of bag you'd carry a suit around in.

She'd graduated from Minegahara in March and was starting college later in April—only one reason she'd have a suit with her.

"Here to show off your outfit for orientation?"

"I had to pick it up now!" Tomoe fumed, hell-bent on denying that she had brought it on purpose. "The shop'll be closed by the time my shift ends!"

"Sure, sure. Might as well put it on, then."

"You're gonna smirk and say I look like a kid playing dress-up."

"Guess I'll see you on the big day. When's the entrance ceremony?"

"Huh? How do you not know that?"

His off-the-cuff question had provoked a weirdly high level of surprise.

What about that was so shocking?

"Why are we assuming I'd know the date of your entrance ceremony?"

He had no memory of discussing it before.

"'Cause we're in the same college?"

"Huh?"

That caught him off guard, and he let out a squeak.

"How is that a huh?" she said, scowling back at him.

"Koga, you're going to some all-girls college in the city, right? You landed a referral and got in without a hitch, and then I bought you wireless earphones to celebrate. I remember that much!"

"You did buy me that present, but we talked about the referral, and I ended up not taking it. I sat exams for your university instead......"

The more she talked, the more worried Tomoe got.

Sakuta was pretty sure he looked every bit as frazzled.

"You really don't remember, Senpai?" Tomoe asked.

It was less doubt and more disbelief.

Sakuta felt exactly the same way. He couldn't bring himself to accept what she was saying. It was too different from what he knew.

"The Koga I knew settled on that girls' college."

"……"

Tomoe was no longer arguing. She just looked lost. And behind that, he caught a clear sign of concern. She clearly thought he'd lost it.

"……"

"……"

Neither knew what else to say.

An uncomfortable silence settled over the cluttered break room.

The awkward tension was broken by someone else entirely.

"Good morning!" said a bright and cheery voice.

Sara Himeji came dancing in. She'd paired a springtime pastel blouse with a rather short skirt.

She found Sakuta and Tomoe in the break room and smiled, saying, "Oh! Sensei! Tomoe-senpai! Good morning to you both!"

"Morning."

"Morning, Himeji."

They both returned the greeting, but their voices betrayed them. Both were acting stiff after that strange conversation.

Sara picked up on that awkwardness and looked at each in turn.

"What's wrong?"

"Nothing. Right, Senpai?"

Tomoe immediately replied to cover for Sakuta.

She seemed to understand he wasn't quite himself and wanted to be considerate.

But Sara was not so easily dismissed.

"Oh yeah? You could cut the air in here with a knife."

Sara shot Tomoe a dubious look.

"Seriously, it's nothing."

"Huh. Fine, be that way."

She must have decided there was nothing to be gained here, and she backed off. Her next words made the reason clear.

"Right, Sakuta-sensei, listen!"

Face brightening, she changed the subject. Clearly eager to spill the beans.

"I saw the best thing at Enoshima yesterday!"

"What?"

"Yamada and Yoshiwa on a date!"

"……"

Sara was almost boasting, and Sakuta failed to react at all. More accurately, it wasn't a surprise for him. He'd heard that story before.

Not in reality.

The source was a dream.

Kento Yamada was a student of his at the cram school, and he'd shared that news at the start of the year. How he'd dreamed of taking another student, Juri Yoshiwa, on a date to Enoshima. A whole puppy-love story. And Sara had dreamed about spotting them on said date.

"So both your dream and Yamada's came true…," he muttered.

"Dream? What dream?" Sara asked, crooking her head.

"You told me about it, right? You dreamed about going to Enoshima with friends and spotting Yamada and Yoshiwa together."

"……"

The whole time he spoke, Sara just looked puzzled. When he was done, she upgraded that to baffled.

Next to her, Tomoe was looking even more concerned.

He was starting to feel cornered.

It was as if some unseen force was tightening around him.

Each breath came less easy than the previous one.

Sakuta felt awful.

Trying to free himself, he sought any glimmer of comprehension.

"Don't act like you don't know. Everyone's taking about dreams coming true."

The more he tried to remain calm, the more panicked he sounded.

"You hear anything like that, Tomoe-senpai?"

"Nope."

Tomoe just shook her head.

"The dreaming hashtag, all over social media!"

His tone was getting stronger. And that made them both tense up.

"Tomoe-senpai, any clues?"

"Sorry, I've got nothing."

She shook her head, clueless.

"......"

Their reaction left Sakuta speechless. It was like his insides had frozen over and the last support holding him up had cracked. He was about to crumble away.

"Hang on, you've never even heard of #dreaming?"

Unable to contain himself, he was leaning forward. His voice was getting louder.

Tomoe and Sara looked at each other. They seemed to be wondering how to handle this.

"Sorry, Senpai," Tomoe said, speaking for them both. "I've got no idea what you're talking about."

"Check your phones. It should be all over all the internet."

They shared another glance, then dutifully pulled out their phones. Clearly used to making these searches. It didn't take long.

"Yep, no such hashtag, Senpai."

"Not on this app, either."

They each showed him their screen, like this proved it.

"That doesn't even…"

Both search results defied his expectations. Not one hit for #dreaming, just fuzzy results.

"Can I borrow that?" Sakuta asked, and he took Tomoe's phone from her to search for the hashtag himself.

He did not get the results he wanted. Just the same outcome she'd shown him.

"……Where'd they all go?"

He tried again.

Naturally, nothing changed.

"Seriously, are you okay?"

He glanced up from the borrowed phone and found Tomoe looking downright scared. Sara was not much better.

Their voices seemed very far away.

They were right here, but it felt like they were a hundred yards away.

His head spun.

"Senpai?"

He was dizzy.

"Sensei?"

He couldn't feel the floor beneath his feet.

"Hey, Senpai…?"

Tomoe and Sara both leaned over.

"Sensei?!"

So did the table and walls. He felt the ceiling falling—then he and his chair toppled over.

There was a loud crash as he hit the floor.

"Eep!" Sara squeaked.

"Senpai!" Tomoe yelped. "Hang in there!"

Ass on the floor, he stared up at the ceiling.

Tomoe was kneeling over him, looking terrified.

Only then did he realize he'd fallen.

"I'm fine. Nothing's wrong."

He raised a hand, trying to prove that.

"You don't fall over if nothing's wrong. If you're sick, you'd better go home."

"I'll call the boss!" Sara said, ducking out through the door.

"I mean that, Senpai. You need to go home right now," Tomoe insisted.

He was starting to think she had a point.

"Thanks, Koga. Maybe I'd better."

Staying here any longer would likely drive him around the bend.

5

"Senpai, be careful getting home."

"Don't take any detours."

Tomoe and Sara sent Sakuta packing, but even outside the restaurant, he remained unsteady on his feet.

It didn't feel like they were on solid ground. Really, he wasn't sure he knew where his feet were, period.

He'd been down this station road so many times, but today it looked unfamiliar. He'd lived here for years but felt like he'd never walked this path before.

Sakuta had this odd sensation that he didn't belong.

Almost as if he'd wandered into a strange new world.

The message from the other Sakuta kept echoing though his mind.

——*Stop Touko Kirishima.*

——*Before reality is rewritten.*

When he combined that with what he was facing, the meaning of it became clear.

"If it was going to be this bad, I wish the other me had been more specific…"

Mai claiming to be Touko Kirishima. Both Kaedes existing at once. Rio and Yuuma dating. Tomoe enrolling in Sakuta's college.

That wasn't the end of it, either.

The dreaming hashtag had caused him no end of problems, but today it was completely gone. He'd certainly wished it would go away sometimes—but not by having it erased from everyone's mind like this.

Too many things different from the world he knew. Too many changes.

If Touko Kirishima was behind all these discrepancies, then he had no choice but to stop her. Getting thrown into this confounding mess meant he had every right to give her a piece of his mind.

But he had no idea who Touko Kirishima was. He'd thought the miniskirt Santa was the real one—until she'd turned out to be someone else. Nene Iwamizawa was never Touko Kirishima.

"But if anyone knows anything, it's Fukuyama's girlfriend…"

Nene had been Touko Kirishima for almost a year. She might hold some clues.

Before he knew it, Sakuta was running from the restaurant to the shopping area by the station.

Was he looking for Touko Kirishima?

Or just running from his fears?

Sakuta wasn't sure, but he knew where he was headed.

Up the stairs to the pedestrian overpass, toward the JR Fujisawa building.

A green pay phone was set in the corner with the coin lockers and kiosks. Sakuta lifted the receiver, dropped in a coin, and dialed a number he'd only just learned.

"Yeah?" A man's voice came on the line.

Takumi Fukuyama, a friend from college.

Only then did Sakuta realize he'd misdialed.

"It's me. Azusagawa."

"Oh, I thought so! It says 'pay phone' so I figured it was you. What's up?"

"Sorry, I meant to call Iwamizawa."

Sakuta was clearly more rattled than he'd thought. But he was in no mood to laugh at himself for it.

"Oh yeah? What for? You okay?"

"I gotta call her so I'll let you go."

"Nah, wait. Nene's with me; lemme pass you over."

In the background, he heard Takumi calling her name, and Sakuta waited a moment.

"What's this about?"

She came on the line, sounding put out.

"Know anything about who Touko Kirishima is?"

"Huh? She's your girlfriend," she scoffed. "I was such a fool. Can't believe I didn't see it."

Her words sounded a bit spiteful, and most of that sentiment seemed reserved for Sakuta.

But he was in no shape to go back and forth on that subject.

"Could you please tell me anything you remember?"

"Seriously, ask your girlfriend."

When he stood his ground, she brushed him off.

"Iwamizawa, you once said something about giving presents. You know, Adolescence Syndrome."

"I might have."

"What did you mean by it?"

"I mean, it seems like listening to Touko Kirishima's songs gave me Adolescence Syndrome. Maybe that's why I thought that?"

Her response almost made it sound like she was just some bystander.

"Maybe I just wanted to convince myself I was special like that."

Her laughter was clearly aimed at herself.

"So you don't know anything else?"

"Nope."

"……"

It was almost anticlimactic how his one hope had been snuffed out.

"Guess I should be grateful," she said. "You helped cure my Adolescence Syndrome. Thanks."

"……You're welcome."

"Wanna talk to Takumi?"

"No, I'm good."

"Yeah? Then bye."

She hung up.

The phone started buzzing, so he set it on the hook. That was when Sakuta realized his hand was shaking.

Everyone was on a different page.

There was no clear path to a solution.

His mouth was dry.

His breathing became fast and shallow as he gasped for air.

He could hear the sounds of the street, but it all seemed so far away.

And yet his heartbeat was weirdly loud. His heart was beating so hard it hurt.

His body was reacting to the terror he felt.

Sakuta recognized this feeling.

He'd experienced this once before.

"Nobody understands me. It's exactly the same."

His third year of junior high.

Nobody had believed that Adolescence Syndrome was real. He'd been isolated.

And right now, he was completely isolated again.

He picked up the receiver with shaking hands.

"Akagi was with me yesterday..."

Ikumi had been shocked when Mai said she was Touko Kirishima. She couldn't believe her ears. Just like Sakuta.

He punched in eleven digits.

But his fingers were trembling so hard he couldn't manage it.

Each time he got one wrong, he had to start over, and it took forever. So many attempts.

The hand holding the receiver was shaking even harder. He had to hold it tight to avoid dropping it, and that only made the tremors worse.

His one stroke of luck was that the call went through quickly.

"Akagi!" he yelled.

But the answer...

"The number you have dialed is not in service. Please check the number and try again."

A flat recorded message.

He must've gotten the number wrong.

That was what he concluded as he dialed again.

Once more, it connected, but all he heard was...

"The number you have dialed is not in service. Please check the number and try again."

The same thing again.

"......"

His brain stopped working.

Unable to process what had happened, he dialed Ikumi's number a third time.

And got that same message.

Sakuta hadn't dialed wrong. He was pretty sure it wasn't a memory issue, either.

But the call wouldn't connect. It wasn't in service.

He could feel a tight knot in his stomach.

It was so agonizing that he found it impossible to stay upright.

Next thing he knew, he was half-collapsed by the pay phone.

No one else to turn to.

He took out his wallet to put the extra coins away...

...and a white scrap of paper slipped out from between the bills within.

"......"

His hands naturally reached for it and pulled it closer.

Eleven digits, written in his hand.

This was his wallet, so Sakuta knew exactly whose number that was.

She'd given it to him two years back.

He knew her name and face.

But he'd never actually dialed it. She'd never tried to call him. They'd stuck to writing letters this whole time.

He put every coin he had into the phone.

Slowly, carefully, he punched in this unfamiliar number.

Making sure he made no mistakes.

Taking deep breaths.

Finally, he hit the last number, and he heard it ringing.

One ring. No pickup.

"……"

A second ring. Silence.

"……"

A third ring came and went—and only then did she answer.

"Hello?"

Her voice sounded just like he'd remembered it.

"Hi, it's been… Sorry to just call out of the blue. It's me. Azusagawa."

He'd utterly failed to prepare an opening remark and wound up spluttering a bit.

She must have found that funny. He heard her giggle.

"Sakuta, your fate is entwined with mine," she said, a teasing lilt in her voice.

He wasn't sure what fate had to do with it.

"……Fate?" he repeated.

He got his answer.

"Behind you."

The voice wasn't from the speaker.

It was right behind him.

"……"

Unable to believe it, Sakuta turned like a windup doll.

Mouth half-open, he found himself face-to-face with a high school girl.

She was three paces away, clad in a Minegahara High uniform.

Her eyes met his, and she broke into a smile, unable to contain her delight.

Sakuta knew this girl.

A special someone from his distant memories.

The high school girl he'd met on the beach at Shichirigahama when he was suffering the most.

She'd comforted him then. His first love.

And now she was standing before him, just as she'd been back then.

His jaw hanging open, he tried to call her name.

——*Shouko.*

But no sounds emerged.

In time, he croaked, "Why…?"

"If I'm going to high school, it's got to be Minegahara!" she said, grinning sheepishly.

Only then did his brain catch up.

"Before school starts, I popped by to talk to the faculty about my body—my heart."

The girl with her hand on her chest was not the girl he'd met at Shichirigahama.

It was the girl who'd moved to Okinawa.

And that girl had graduated from junior high and was about to start high school this spring. It all added up.

"So what do you think? Does the uniform look good?"

She struck a pose.

"Makinohara!" Sakuta said, unable to stop himself.

Shouko looked somewhat taken aback.

But she soon flashed a happy grin.

"I'm right here, Sakuta!" she said. "And now that I'm here, it's all gonna be okay."

"……Is it?"

"Let's go meet Touko Kirishima together."

Chapter 3
A Butterfly Flaps Its Wings

1

The next day was Monday, April 3.

Sakuta was behind the wheel of a rental car, driving on the Tomei Expressway, speed limit sixty-five miles per hour. An hour or so ago, they'd crossed the prefectural border between Kanagawa and Shizuoka and had just now passed Fuji City. They'd left Fujisawa almost two hours back.

He'd driven this far without getting bored because the view of Mount Fuji was beautiful, and because of the high school girl sitting in the passenger seat. The same one he'd been reunited with the previous day.

"How's Nasuno doing?" Shouko asked, nibbling on some Pocky. She offered Sakuta one.

He munched on that, then answered. "She's great. Steps on my face to wake me up in the morning. How's Hayate?"

"Great. He got so big. I'll show you some photos later."

She sounded delighted. But her eyes were on the blue-and-white road signs.

"We're almost in Makinohara."

She pointed proudly at the sign bearing her name.

"Can we stop in the rest area on the way back? I wanna grab some souvenirs for my parents."

"I don't mind stopping, but first…can you share where we're going?"

Sakuta might be driving, but he was unaware of their destination. Shouko had told him nothing.

"You'll find out when we get there," she said, impishly pressing a Pocky to her lips. She alone knew their destination and had been helping him navigate this whole time. The phone in her hand had replaced the car's built-in GPS.

He caught glimpses of the map on her screen, but from the driver's seat, he couldn't make out where they were headed.

"Then can I ask why you're in uniform?"

"I thought this would do it for you," she said, grinning.

Shouko in a Minegahara uniform was visually indistinguishable from the other Shouko, his first love.

"I dunno about doing it for me, but it's certainly doing a number on me. Shouko used to be older than me, but now she's turned into the younger Makinohara."

He had to laugh, but he meant every word.

An older high school girl he met years ago should have gone on to college. She'd have joined the workforce by now. And yet here she was again, sitting next to him, back in high school and several years younger than he was.

The one thing that hadn't changed was the smile on her face. She watched him drive with a tender look in her eyes.

"You've starting to look grown-up, Sakuta."

"Well, I can drive now."

"And I'm in uniform because that's how high school students dress up."

"You're taking me somewhere formal enough to have a dress code? Is that why you said to dress nice today?"

He hadn't exactly rolled up in the starched suit he'd worn to the college entrance ceremony, but he did have a jacket on over his T-shirt. Business casual? It looked decent enough, he thought.

"Don't worry, you look good in that, Sakuta."

"We're going to see Touko Kirishima, right?"

"We are."

"Armed with gifts."

He glanced in the rear-view mirror. There was a bag of dove cookies in the back. Shouko had brought them for Touko Kirishima.

"Yep. Oh, take the next interchange."

They must have been getting closer.

Off the expressway, they followed a national highway south.

The first ten minutes were mostly green. Occasional isolated houses surrounded by tea fields. Very pastoral.

Around the twenty-minute mark, they started to see larger buildings: processing plants.

Five minutes after they'd passed a factory with the name of a famous tea company emblazoned on the side, the farms had given way to a town.

"Turn left at the next corner," Shouko said, eyes on the map on her phone.

"Got it."

He made the turn.

Shouko's back left the seat, and she began peering out the driver's-side window. It wasn't long before she spotted their destination.

"Stop at the florist," she said.

There was indeed a sign bedecked with flowers.

Making sure there were no cars behind them or oncoming, Sakuta pulled into the lot.

He put the parking brake on and killed the engine.

"This won't take long, Sakuta. You wait in the car."

Without waiting for an answer, Shouko opened the door and hopped out.

He turned back, and she was already stepping into the shop, calling out to the staff. They spoke briefly, and she did come right back out.

"Thanks for waiting," Shouko said, settling into the passenger seat with a bouquet.

Nothing weird about stopping by a flower shop.

But the type of bouquet caught his attention.

"The orange are marigolds, the long white ones are stock, the pale purple are sweet pea, and the yellow are freesia."

He hadn't asked, but Shouko told him anyway, her tone unchanged. Each flower was beautiful on its own, but bundled together like this, it was all too obvious what this bouquet was for.

Pretty much everyone in Japan would recognize that color combo at a glance.

Flowers for the dead.

Sakuta's gaze shifted from the bouquet to her face as she put her seatbelt on.

"Head right," Shouko said, looking straight ahead.

"Okay."

Choosing not to pry further, he started the car.

They drove maybe fifty yards.

"We're almost there. I'll tell you everything when we arrive," Shouko whispered.

"If we're almost there, then I can wait that long."

Maintaining a safe distance from the car ahead, Sakuta pressed the gas pedal, speeding up.

Five minutes later, Shouko gave the word, and they stopped in the lot outside an old, historical-looking temple.

2

Passing under a magnificent two-story gate, Shouko and Sakuta entered the temple grounds. No one else was around; the place was shrouded in a solemn silence.

They started by paying their respects in the main hall.

Once that was over, Shouko said, "It's this way," and led the way to the back of the grounds.

Ahead he could see a graveyard.

There was a trough, and they filled a bucket at it. Sakuta carried the pail, following Shouko through the rows of gravestones. The only sounds were their footsteps…and the water sloshing in the bucket.

From behind, Shouko looked a bit tense.

Sakuta himself was taking deep breaths, unconsciously trying to settle his nerves.

At last, Shouko stopped before a grave.

"……"

Silently checking something.

"I think this is it," she whispered.

"You think? Your first time here, then?"

"Yeah."

The inscription merely contained a dedication to their ancestors, nothing to indicate who slept here.

But he could guess.

Sakuta knew why they'd come all this way. Shouko had invited him to go see Touko Kirishima and then brought him here.

That was all he needed.

So without further questions, he put his hands together. Shouko already had.

In silence, they cleared away the weeds, rinsed the stone, and placed the flowers on the grave. They filled the water basin. Shouko pulled some incense out of her bag; they each lit half and laid it down.

Once again, they closed their eyes, hands together.

"......"

"......"

When Sakuta raised his head, Shouko was still praying. When he studied her features, he detected emotions that were impossible to describe in a few simple words.

Gratitude was first and foremost.

But she wasn't just thankful.

The length of the silence made that painfully obvious.

At last, her eyes came up and found Sakuta. She started with a wan sort of smile, but that gradually grew earnest. Her eyes fell on the list of names placed next to the grave.

Sakuta followed her gaze.

This stone was engraved with the names of those resting here.

He followed it from right to left, the years becoming more recent.

At the far left, the newest entry...

Only sixteen when she died.

Four years ago. December 24.

And the name...Touko Kirishima.

"Christmas Eve, four years ago," Shouko said softly. "She went out to see a friend and was hit by a car."

"......"

"They called an ambulance, and she was taken to the hospital, but she never woke up."

"……"

"And they found a donor card in her belongings."

He didn't have to hear the rest.

But Sakuta waited for Shouko to finish.

Her eyes locked on Touko Kirishima's name as she continued.

"It was Touko Kirishima who became my donor."

He'd seen this coming when she'd brought him here.

"……"

But hearing it from Shouko's lips left him speechless. His heart was unsure how to take this news. He was at a loss.

They'd come to see Touko Kirishima and learned she had already passed. The truth—she'd saved Shouko's life where Mai and Sakuta could not.

All this time he'd assumed she was a total stranger, but she'd had a huge impact on his life. On Mai's and Shouko's as well.

And this revelation left him reeling.

"Sakuta, I once told you…"

"……"

He turned his eyes her way, probing.

"There was no artist named Touko Kirishima in any future I experienced."

That sounded familiar.

"You said that before you moved to Okinawa."

Shouko nodded.

"I believe that's because every future I saw, I had either your heart or Mai's."

There was a light in her eyes that said more than her words possibly could. Sakuta wasn't about to miss what that meant.

"In other words, 'Touko Kirishima' started uploading videos *because* we changed the future?"

"It adds up, right?"

"But she's already gone. Ever since Christmas Eve, four years ago."

The numbers on that list were undeniable.

"And 'Touko Kirishima' started taking off, like, two years back. That doesn't make sense. She's not a ghost, is she?"

"That's why I invited you to join me here. I wanted to know more about the girl who gave me a future."

Shouko was very serious about this.

He could see more than just gratitude in her eyes. A hint of sorrow. A tearful smile, at peace, yet tinged with grief.

"I imagined you'd feel the same way."

"You're even talking like my Shouko now."

That got a laugh out of her.

But her smile soon faded. Her gaze shifted behind him—to the graveyard's entrance.

Sakuta heard footsteps and turned to find a woman coming their way, carrying flowers and a bucket. She was in her midforties.

She spotted the two of them and bobbed her head. They bowed back.

"Shouko Makinohara, right?" she asked hesitantly.

"That's right. I'm Shouko Makinohara."

"Thanks for coming all this way to see Touko. I'm her mother."

She bowed low again.

"Thank you for answering my letters. Thank you very much."

Shouko bowed low herself.

Her words of gratitude seemed to carry so much weight.

And that prevented Sakuta from sticking his oar in. He wasn't needed here. There was a hint of tension between Shouko and Touko's mother, each holding back. They were both measuring the distance between them. But with a real warmth behind them that overrode all of that.

Each putting the other first.

3

"Thanks for the lovely flowers. I'm sure Touko's delighted."

Touko's mother joined them in paying her respects, then said this was no place to talk and invited them over to her house.

Sakuta and Shouko climbed into their rental and followed Touko's mother's car. On the way, Shouko filled Sakuta in.

"After the heart transplant, I sent letters to the donor's family through a support organization. I wrote a lot about my life. How I started my second year of junior high, went to the beach, how tall I was getting…"

"But you didn't know the donor's name?"

"No. I wasn't even sure the family had agreed to accept the letters. It can't have been easy for them."

"But it's very you to keep sending them anyway, Makinohara."

He meant that.

"Last month, after high school entrance exams, I wrote a letter saying I'd been admitted to the school I'd wanted to go to. 'If I hadn't received a heart transplant, I would never have become a high school student at all.'"

Shouko spoke softly, her voice tender. Brimming with gratitude. Just listening to her filled Sakuta's heart with warmth, and he had to fight off tears. There was a persistent tingle right behind his nose.

"And that got you an answer?"

"Her mother wrote back. She'd read every letter I sent. That's when

I found out my donor had also been a first-year high school girl and her name was Touko Kirishima."

He didn't need her to spell out the rest. That reply had led to them writing back and forth directly, and to today's visit.

The car in front of them turned off onto a side street. Sakuta turned his blinker on and made the same turn.

Not five minutes later, their cars pulled up to a farmhouse with a barn built next to it.

Outside the car, their noses caught a distinct fragrance.

"Wow, you can really smell the tea," Shouko said.

"Like the letter said, we're tea growers," Touko's mother said. She led them inside the house. "Make yourselves at home."

"Thank you."

"Thanks."

Sakuta followed Shouko inside.

They were led down a hall of lovely hardwood to a living room about ten tatami mats large. From the recessed space, they had a great view of the area between the house and the barn. You could easily park four or five cars there.

There was an altar on the side of the room.

"Um, I brought these," Shouko said, handing over the dove cookies.

"That's so nice of you. Touko loved these. She'll love them. I'll go put the kettle on; you wait here."

"Do you mind if we pay our respects?"

"Not at all. Go right ahead."

They waited for the mother to leave, then knelt down before the altar. They lit the candle, then each lit an incense stick. Shouko rang the bell, and Sakuta closed his eyes, putting his palms together.

He held that longer than he had at the grave.

Adding in gratitude for saving Shouko's life.

The mother came back in with a teapot and kettle. First, she put some cookies on the altar.

Then she made tea for Sakuta and Shouko.

"Thank you for coming all this way to see Touko," she said, repeatedly bowing her head.

"Not at all. I wanted to see her. Thank you for having me."

Shouko did the same.

"I just couldn't bring myself to write back for the longest time," the mother said, eyes on the table.

"I was so happy you did," Shouko said. "I was worried my letters were unwelcome."

"At first…well, it took me a while to feel up to it. As time went on, I remembered more things…and I came to believe it was a good thing she went to a girl like you, Shouko."

A tear ran down her cheek.

"Oh, pardon me," she said, turning away and wiping her eyes.

All Sakuta could do was sit and watch. There was nothing for him to say here. That went for Shouko, too. They simply waited for the moment to pass.

"You've done nothing wrong, Shouko. I'm so, so sorry. Please, drink up before it gets cold."

She smiled through her tears.

"Thank you."

Shouko took a sip.

"That's so good!"

"I'm glad you think so."

The mother smiled and wiped her eyes again.

Sakuta took a sip himself. The tea had a gentle fragrance, with a bite beneath it. A hint of sweetness revealed itself at the end.

"Did Touko drink this tea a lot?" Sakuta asked, his first time speaking since they came in.

"Honestly, she never really had a taste for it," her mother said with a chuckle. "When I asked if she wanted any, she usually said no. She and my husband argued about it a lot. 'You don't want the tea your mother makes?!' Oh, he's not here, I'm afraid. I told him you were coming, Shouko, but he just said 'Gonna check the fields' and went out."

Sakuta couldn't exactly say he knew how that felt, but he could imagine the man didn't know what to do with himself around the girl who'd received his daughter's heart. Like Touko's mom said, it wasn't Shouko's fault. But seeing her was a forceful reminder of his daughter, and her absence—and memories from when she'd still lived. It might just hurt him—and he might just hurt Shouko. In which case, better not to see her at all.

"I feel like I'm doing all the talking."

"No, go right ahead," Shouko said. "I'm here to learn more about Touko. Please, tell me more."

"In that case, let me show you her room. It's just how she left it."

The look on the mother's face was equal parts glad and sad.

"I know someday I'll have to pack it all up, but...," she said, almost making excuses.

She got up, and they followed after her into the hall and upstairs.

Touko's room was at the back of the second floor.

"Go on in," her mother said. Sakuta followed Shouko inside.

It must have been the size of eight tatami mats, a bit larger than the average bedroom.

No real furniture besides the bed and desk—a pretty basic layout.

There was a small bookcase on the desk, and Shouko let out a little noise.

She pulled a Blu-ray disc off the shelf.

Someone Sakuta knew well was on the cover.

Mai.

Mai Sakurajima, in her junior high years.

This movie had been a huge hit.

She'd played a girl waiting for a heart transplant.

"That movie turned Touko into a die-hard fan. She was always buying fashion magazines for photos of her."

The mother pulled open a drawer. Inside were magazines with Mai on the cover. All in great shape—Touko had clearly taken care of them. She had cared enough to store them in her desk drawer.

"And she loved music."

After closing the drawer, the mother turned to the acoustic guitar by the mirror. With so little clutter, both Sakuta and Shouko had spotted it right away.

"She wrote her own songs, too. On the computer."

"I don't see a computer," Shouko said.

The desk was largely empty. There were speakers on either side of it, attached to nothing—a conspicuous gap in the center.

"A good friend of hers asked for it. She still has it."

At that, Shouko shot Sakuta a meaningful glance.

"Oh, I've got some photos! Take a look."

Before they could ask about this friend, the mother moved on. She pulled an album from a shelf full of textbooks and dictionaries.

And laid it down for them to see.

Touko was very young in the first pages. Likely starting preschool.

Dressed in an adorable uniform, looking ready to bounce off the walls. Holding her mother's hand.

The next page had more preschool photos. Another girl in uniform was with Touko. They'd made origami, and Touko was showing it to the camera. The girl next to her was staring fixedly at the crane in her hand.

"This is the friend I mentioned. They got to know each other in preschool and stayed friends through elementary, junior high, and high school."

As she turned the pages, this played out. There was a photo of their first day of elementary school. Touko with a red knapsack on, standing next to that other little girl outside the gates.

Each time the page turned, those two girls showed up.

At the aquarium—a field trip?

Photos from the school trip, smiling at their graduation ceremony…

They stood together at the entrance ceremony for junior high, were dressed as monsters for the culture festival, had matching face paint for the sports festival…

On every page, Touko was with this friend.

And as Sakuta looked, as the pages turned, as the two girls grew up…disbelief began to swell within him.

His eyes were caught less by Touko than by her friend.

She looked like someone he knew.

His mind playing tricks?

He kept telling himself that it made no sense.

But as the girls got older, he could no longer deny it.

Touko's friend looked just like *her*.

"……"

He reached for the page and found his hand shaking.

His mouth was dry as a bone.

By the time he flipped to the junior high graduation, he was almost certain.

He knew the girl in the photos with Touko.

"How can that be?"

Unable to stop himself, lips quivering with surprise—the words slipped out. He could tell he'd gone white as a sheet.

"Sakuta?" Shouko asked, puzzled and concerned.

"I think I know her."

He pointed to the girl at Touko's side.

"Oh?" Shouko said with surprise. She'd seen a lot of different futures but must not have expected a coincidence like this.

Sakuta himself found it hard to believe.

There was no room for doubt, yet he still found himself saying, "Probably." To turn that into certainty, he flipped another page.

That brought him to the two girls in high school.

Likely taken outside this very house.

Touko was in her brand-new uniform, grinning, throwing a peace sign at the camera. Her friend was doing the same pose, clearly roped into it.

And the look on her face was all too familiar.

She still wore her hair half up.

He spotted the teardrop mole beneath her left eye.

She looked just a bit younger than the girl he knew.

But she was now old enough that he could not refute it.

"Mitou…"

The name of a potential friend from college crossed his lips.

"Oh? You know Miori?" Touko's mother asked, looking surprised.

"Yeah, we go to the same college."

Sakuta was far more shocked than she was and barely managed a reply.

She asked something else, and he said something in return, but wholly on autopilot. No conscious thought was involved. Shock had filled every crevice of his brain.

"Touko Kirishima" was the last person he'd expected.

Someone so close by.

Miori Mitou.

4

Three o'clock came and went, and Touko's father never came back from the fields. Given the length of the drive home, they left at half past three.

"I *am* sorry. He really can't handle these things."

The mother shook her head.

"Don't worry about it," Shouko said, smiling softly. "If you've no objections, I'd like to come visit Touko again."

"By all means. Oh, please take this."

The mother was starting to mist up again, but she handed Shouko a little bag. It was packed full of tea.

"Thank you so much."

"Also…" She handed something else over.

A notebook.

"What's this…?"

"An exchange diary. Touko and Miori…the friend I mentioned? They traded it back and forth. I thought it might help you get to know her better."

"Are you sure…?"

Standing next to her, Sakuta could feel Shouko's trepidation through his skin.

An exchange diary would be stuffed full of Touko's unvarnished thoughts. They knew this must be hard for her mother to let go of.

"Of course. If you don't object…"

"I'll take good care of it. And I swear I'll bring it back."

Sakuta took the bag of tea, and Shouko accepted the exchange diary. Despite how slim the notebook was, it seemed heavy in her hands.

"We'd better get going."

They bobbed their heads one last time and climbed into the car.

Touko's mother waved, and Shouko bowed her head low. Sakuta gave them time for one last goodbye before he started driving.

After checking both ways, he pulled out onto the road and gradually reached the speed limit.

No cars ahead or behind.

For a while, they had the road to themselves, and they drove along in silence.

The whole time, Shouko sat in the passenger seat, her eyes on the cover of the exchange diary.

Touko and Miori.

Their names were on the cover, in their respective handwriting.

She made no attempt to open it and read. Even after accepting the notebook, Shouko seemed deeply unsure it was right for her to look inside.

In time, they reached the national road. They headed for the expressway entrance.

The farther they drove, the fewer houses they saw. Soon it was only tea fields.

"Her mother chose to entrust you with that, Makinohara. It's safe to look."

"Yeah."

She nodded but still made no move to open it. Instead, she placed it carefully in her bookbag, making sure it wouldn't be damaged.

"Once I'm home, I'll take my time with it."

"Sounds like a plan."

To Shouko, these were the words of the benefactor who'd granted her a future. She'd want to treasure every last one.

"Her mom seemed nice," he said, changing the subject.

The expressway came into view.

"Yeah, very nice."

The tears had welled up in the kind woman's eyes several times while talking about Touko, and that had stuck with them. It was plain to see she'd done everything she could to act cheery in front of them.

And seeing that firsthand had to have been especially hard on Shouko.

"……"

He figured that's why she was so quiet.

"You did nothing wrong, Makinohara."

"……That's not necessarily true," she said, with a rueful smile.

Sakuta pretended not to catch that look. He focused on the road.

"Sakuta, you know the fable about the butterfly that flaps its wings and causes a tornado somewhere else?" Shouko asked, her voice subdued.

"The butterfly effect? Futaba mentioned it once."

"What starts as a small change can eventually become a very significant one."

Shouko leaned against the passenger-side window. He could see her thoughtful expression reflected in it.

"Sure, but unless you're Laplace's demon, there's no way to go from the result to the original root cause. Futaba said so. No one can know what really causes anything."

He *did* know a petite devil, but Tomoe's calculations applied exclusively to the future.

"So you did nothing wrong, Makinohara."

As he said it, he turned onto the expressway ramp.

Shouko offered no response at all.

Sakuta sped up, merging into the sixty-five-mile-per-hour traffic.

"Are you okay, Sakuta?"

"Why wouldn't I be?"

"That stuff about Miori Mitou."

"It sure came outta nowhere. Caught me by surprise."

He meant that.

"But this means Mitou is definitely the real Touko Kirishima."

"I think so, yeah." Shouko nodded.

"She did say she can't stand karaoke."

He recalled the first day he met her. Everyone at the party they attended had decided to head for karaoke, and they'd bailed together.

"You think this is why?"

"That's the kind of excuse Mitou would make."

If she started singing, people might notice.

She was probably great at karaoke but had to pretend she wasn't and make light of it.

"If 'Touko Kirishima' is rewriting reality, then that means this whole mess is Mitou's fault."

If he trusted the message from the other potential world, that is. But blaming her just didn't feel right. And Shouko soon put one reason for that into words.

"What's Miori really after?"

He really didn't have a clue.

"I think I get the part where she'd sing using her friend's name."

"Making Touko unforgettable. Letting her name alone live on," Shouko said.

Sakuta nodded. "But now everyone thinks 'Touko Kirishima' was Mai all along, and Mai herself said as much."

"Do you think she rewrote reality that way because the real Touko was a big Mai fan?"

"Can't rule it out…"

But that theory also didn't quite fit, which gave him pause.

"You seem unconvinced."

"I've just never felt anything like that from Mitou. No strong convictions or beliefs from what I could see."

That's why it didn't make sense that she was rewriting things.

"What's she like?" Shouko asked.

"Hard to get a read on. She always keeps herself just out of reach."

"Like a mirage?"

"Maybe."

He let out a laugh. An apt turn of phrase.

"But that makes one thing clear," Shouko said.

"Does it?"

"Miori Mitou is exactly the type of person you go for, Sakuta."

She flashed a triumphant grin.

"I said nothing like that. The only person who's my type is Mai."

"And also me."

Shouko stuck out her tongue, and he grimaced.

"Oh, you wanted to stop at this rest area," he said, switching to the left lane.

The first thing Shouko did was take a selfie by the Makinohara Rest Area sign. Then they perused the offerings in the gift shop. The area was known for tea, and they had lots of tea-related stuff to choose from. Shouko wound up buying a roll cake, and Sakuta bought some pudding for Kaede.

"Sakuta, let's have some of that," Shouko said, pointing, and they each bought some soft serve. Shouko went with a mix of green tea and milk flavors. Sakuta went with *houjicha*.

This rest stop had a dog run. Not something you saw every day. There were several dogs happily racing around as the skies tipped toward evening.

Watching them go, Sakuta voiced a thought.

"There's no do-overs like with us."

Even if there were, and Touko survived…there was no telling what would happen to Shouko. Chances were there'd be a future where she didn't make it.

"We're in the present now, so that's not possible."

"I thought so."

She was right.

They'd managed to change things because that timeline had always been the future. They'd been able to return from the future to the present. But there was no way to go from the present to the past. He remembered Rio explaining why that was so much harder.

"Which means I've just gotta go see Mitou empty-handed."

He took a bite of soft serve. Each bite filled his mouth with the nutty flavors of the *houjicha*.

"Want to read the exchange diary, Sakuta?"

He considered that.

"……I'd better not," he said, shaking his head.

"It might provide some insight."

Shouko sounded concerned.

"I'll be fine."

He didn't hesitate. He wasn't super sure what he meant by *fine*. But he was weirdly sure about how to approach Miori.

"I figured it was high time we actually became friends."

"Even if it's my fault Touko died?"

"Even if it was *my* fault Touko Kirishima died, I'd still wanna be Mitou's friend."

With that, he popped the last bite of the waffle cone into his mouth.

Sakuta and Shouko pulled out of the rest area at half past four. The skies in the west were just starting to turn red.

The car soon got up to speed, sweeping them along at sixty-five miles per hour. Roughly two hours later, at six thirty, they were back in Fujisawa.

Before returning the rental, he stopped by his apartment building, intending to drop off Shouko and the gifts they'd bought.

As he did, he spotted a familiar white minivan outside the building across the street. It belonged to Mai's manager, Ryouko Hanawa.

"Looks like Mai just got back."

He hadn't seen her since the bus serving as her greenroom at the music festival.

When Sakuta got out, the rear door of the minivan slid open, and Mai hopped out. She must have spotted him from inside. She came over, not looking at all surprised. She had a hint of grump around her eyes—and he knew why.

"Why does Shouko get a lift before I do?" she grumbled, pinching both his cheeks and pulling them apart.

"Sakuta did nothing wrong! I begged him to spend the day with me!" Shouko declared, before he could make any excuses.

Mai's gaze turned to her.

"......"

"......"

Their eyes met, and a silence fell. A tense one.

But only for a moment.

"Welcome back, Shouko."

"It's nice to be back."

The shadow over them passed.

"The Minegahara uniform looks good on you."

"I'm enjoying it quite a bit. Lets me wrap Sakuta around my finger."

"You're even talking like the older Shouko now."

Her rapid growth left Mai somewhat perturbed.

"Mai," a voice called from behind her. "I'm gonna take your stuff up to your room."

It was her manager, Ryouko. She dragged a suitcase out of the van and headed to the door.

"No, I'll handle it. You go on home, Ryouko. Get some rest."

Mai took a few steps away, then turned back.

"Shouko, we'll have to catch up soon," she said.

"Sure."

"Sakuta, make sure she gets home."

"I planned on it. If that won't piss you off?"

"Rest assured, I'm livid."

She flashed a smile, then took her suitcase from her manager, waved at Shouko and Sakuta again, and vanished into the building. He watched until she was out of sight.

Ryouko got back in the van, bobbed her head at Sakuta, and drove off. She turned left at the corner and was soon in the wind.

That left just the two of them.

"You are loved, Sakuta."

"I know."

"Mai was certainly acting like herself."

"Other than claiming to be Touko Kirishima, she is."

"And that's what's got you so rattled?"

"She's Mai, but not."

"And also not Mai, but she is?"

Shouko had him dead to rights.

"Either way, the ball's in Miori Mitou's court," Shouko added.

Right she was. For that reason, Sakuta settled for nodding.

"It sure is," he said.

5

Thursday, April 6.

A sunny day.

The air felt fresh—they'd just welcomed a whole new crop of students to the campus located a convenient three-minute walk from Kanazawa-hakkei Station.

Orientation had been the day before, and the freshmen were beset with invites from clubs and teams along the gingko lane.

"I guess they did this last year, too…," Sakuta muttered, one eye on that bustle as he headed to the main building.

This was the first day back for sophomores, and all he had was an orientation for statistical science majors.

He was about to step into the third-floor class when he heard footsteps running up behind him.

"Good morning, Sakuta!" a cheery voice cried.

Only one person got that bright and lively.

Puzzled by it, Sakuta turned around.

"Let's make it a good one!" Uzuki said, beaming at him.

"Why are you here, Zukki?"

"We've got orientation!"

"Didn't you drop out of college so you could dual-wield a solo career and Sweet Bullet?"

"I told you this. I'm doing both *and* going to college! Triple wielding!"

Sakuta had no such memory.

Uzuki had left school last fall for the reasons he'd stated.

"Good morning, everybody!" Uzuki cried, being very much herself. Oblivious to his consternation. She jogged off to join a group of girls.

Nobody seemed baffled by her presence. She clearly belonged here.

There wasn't much point in letting this trip him up, so he simply followed her in.

Takumi spotted him and raised a hand.

"Yo, Fukuyama," Sakuta said, settling down next to him.

"Mm?"

"What's your take on Hirokawa?"

His eyes were on the far end of the room, where Uzuki was chatting with the other girls.

"I think she's cute."

A breezy answer.

Takumi clearly had no questions about Uzuki's presence here. Like the rest of the students, he thought she belonged.

Reality had been rewritten. This wasn't the world Sakuta knew.

"Yo, Fukuyama."

"What now?"

"I hear you shouldn't call other girls cute when you've got a girlfriend."

"Don't tell Nene."

"If you buy me lunch."

As they kept up their idle banter, Sakuta felt eyes on him. Their curiosity was palpable. He knew why. This was about the events of the April 1 music festival.

"So did you know all along, Azusagawa?"

"I did not."

"Huh? What?"

"You mean Mai being Touko Kirishima, yeah?"

"Can you read minds?"

"That happened once, temporarily."

"Hah? Now you're scaring me."

Takumi recoiled, covering his chest with both arms. Apparently, he believed the mind was in the heart.

"I'm kidding."

"I figured," Takumi laughed, like he always did.

At this point, the white-haired professor came in.

Chatter died down, and students took their seats.

There were no well-intentioned preambles—the statistical science orientation got right down to business. The professor mostly spoke about their attitudes and the program direction.

"You'll be attending more lectures in your major, so if you failed any of the core curriculum classes, be sure to make those up before the year is out."

"Did you blow any, Azusagawa?" Takumi whispered.

"I'm not you, so no."

"I didn't fail any, either!"

* * *

The statistical science orientation was scheduled for a full ninety minutes but was compressed quite a bit and over in thirty. That left Sakuta free by eleven AM.

The other students were filing out, friends asking one another what classes they planned to sign up for.

They had a grace period of ten days to pick which classes they'd be taking in the first semester. A big difference from high school—they had to figure out their own schedules. Furiously studying a list of classes, each with something dubbed a syllabus—what language was that word, anyway?

He'd been through this process twice already in his first year, and it had been fraught. But today especially his mind just refused to process these blocks of time.

He had stuff to do.

"Any plans, Azusagawa?"

"You and your girlfriend got that campus date, right?"

"Ah-ha, I see you've made plans, too."

Takumi acted like he saw right through him, and he spoke like it, too. He'd read way too much into his question, but Sakuta didn't see the point in correcting him.

"Then I'm outta here," Takumi said, shouldering his bookbag.

Belatedly, Sakuta got to his feet, psyched himself up, and put his arms through the straps of his rucksack.

Outside class, he started wandering the building, scoping out the other classrooms. Most majors had wrapped up their orientations, and only a few scattered stragglers remained. He didn't see Miori among them.

Sakuta went down the stairs to the second floor and ran into a different familiar face.

"Oh, Senpai."

Tomoe looked surprised to see him.

He knew the girl next to her, too. Tomoe's friend Nana Yoneyama.

"You came here, too, Yoneyama?"

"Hah? This again, Senpai? I told you we both passed together!"

"Oh, maybe you did."

He didn't remember that, but best to play along.

"Oh, right, Senpai, what's good in the cafeteria? We're headed there now."

"Gotta be the *yokoichi-don*."

"Should we go with that?" Tomoe asked Nana.

Nana gave a little nod.

"That place fills up quick in spring. Better hurry."

"Really? Okay, let's hurry, Nana."

"Oh, wait, Tomoe!"

Nana bobbed her head at Sakuta and raced off down the stairs after her friend.

They were soon out of earshot.

"Koga really *is* at this school," he muttered.

He clearly remembered her getting a referral to an all-girls school in the city…but the facts as he knew them and the reality before him did not match up.

"Is this all Mitou's fault?"

"Is what all my fault?"

A voice from right behind him.

He flinched despite himself.

And slowly swung around.

The girl he'd been looking for.

"Mitou, can we talk?"

"Can you make it short?"

"I'd rather make it long."

"I'm up for anything nonromantic."

They were interrupted by a growling stomach. Miori's stomach.

"I'm hungry, so should we chat while we eat?" Sakuta offered.

"The cafeteria's packed. Let's just grab something and eat in the garden," Miori said, not batting an eye.

She was already on the move.

There were several others in the main building's center garden, but they found an open picnic table. Sakuta and Miori took seats on opposite sides of the table, armed with bottled tea and sandwiches from a convenience store.

First, they unwrapped the sandwiches and filled themselves up. Miori was opening her mouth wide, happily wolfing it down.

The garden was drenched in spring sunshine.

There was a man-made lake with a bridge over it, and on a rock in the middle, a rather large turtle was happily drying its shell.

A peaceful lunchtime.

"So, Mitou."

"What?"

"Wanna rent a car and go for a drive this weekend?"

In response to his suggestion, Miori first blinked twice, saying nothing. Then she flashed a vicious smirk.

"Sounds like a line for your girlfriend," she said pointedly.

"Mai's real busy. She's gotta be Touko Kirishima now."

"Everyone's talking about that."

Miori glanced at the table next to them, where four girls sat, peering at a phone lying on the center of the table. They could just make out a Touko Kirishima song. The girls were laughing and chatting, the names Touko Kirishima and Mai Sakurajima floating on the breeze.

"So if your girlfriend's unavailable, best to invite another friend who's got a license."

"Does that apply to potential friends?" Miori asked. She was smiling.

"Mitou, to your mind, where does 'friend' begin?"

"I feel like taken men asking another girl on a drive rules it out."

"I'm asking where the border of friendship lies, not the border of infidelity."

"Azusagawa," Miori said, before he'd even finished. The mood changed in an instant.

"What?"

"You ever kill anyone?"

The tone of her voice hadn't changed at all. But the question blindsided him.

"……"

He failed to find the words.

"I have. On Christmas Eve, my first year of high school."

Still, her tone stayed the same.

Her expression never wavered.

Her eyes stayed on the turtle sunning itself.

"A friend of mine was supposed to come over. I was waiting at home for her, and she texted me. 'At the store, what you want?' I wrote back, 'Curry bun!' A minute later, she sent 'Curry bun acquired!' But I waited and waited, and she never showed up. I texted, 'Where are you?' and it never got marked read. A car had run a red light and hit my friend."

Not once did an emotion cross Miori's face. Her expression as still as the turtle on that rock.

"You think if you hadn't asked for a curry bun, your friend wouldn't have been run over?"

"She'd have gotten through the line that much faster."

Maybe.

Maybe not.

Sakuta hadn't been there; he couldn't know for sure.

All he knew was that Miori's friend had lost her life in the accident.

"That friend was Touko Kirishima," he said, looking right at her.

"……"

She didn't seem surprised.

"You were 'Touko Kirishima' all along."

Still no real reaction.

And she soon told him why.

"I got a letter yesterday. From Touko's mom. She said a high school girl came to visit, with a college boy in tow. That's why, Azusagawa."

"Why what?"

"Why we can never be friends."

Miori looked at him and smiled. A beautiful smile that would make most men fall for her. But to Sakuta's eyes, it looked impossibly fragile and delicate. She seemed like she might shatter any minute now. That's what made it beautiful. Like cherry blossoms. The kind of smile that rejected anyone and anything.

A bell rang. Lunchtime was almost over.

Miori took that as her cue to stand up.

"I've got a shift, so I'd better go," she said, and she walked off toward the main gates.

"Mitou," Sakuta said, getting up and calling after her.

She didn't pause. Didn't even look back.

Sakuta didn't let that bother him.

He just kept talking.

"Saturday. Meet me at the gates of Ofuna Station at noon."

Miori's back gave him no answer.

Not even a flicker of response.

In time, she vanished through the gates and out of Sakuta's line of sight.

6

After Miori left, Sakuta headed for the library. He printed out syllabi he thought he'd need and went home.

The gingko lane was still packed with clubs recruiting freshmen. Sakuta blew past that commotion and out the gates.

"There you are," said the last person he expected.

Saki Kamisato was glaring at him. She was Yuuma's girlfriend—well, ex-girlfriend.

"Have you heard from Ikumi?" she asked, before he could say a word.

"Akagi? I thought the nursing program moved to the Fukuura campus for the second year?"

"That's why I'm waiting here! I can't get in touch with her. She hasn't been to classes."

"Oh?"

"She's not reading any messages I sent, and if I call, it says the number's out of service."

He remembered getting the same message the last time he tried to call.

"Since when?"

"Since the night of the first. That morning, she said she was going to the festival with you."

"That's the last time I saw her."

Less than a week had passed since then. It was pretty common for him to go a week or two without seeing her. He hadn't noticed anything wrong.

"So you know nothing, Azusagawa?" Saki asked, equal parts anxious and irritated.

"I don't know anything. If I get in touch with her, I'll tell her you're worried."

"Okay. Do that."

With that, Saki spun on her heel and stalked off toward the station.

"Hey, Kamisato," Sakuta called after her.

"What?"

She stopped and turned around, clearly put out.

"Why'd you join the nursing program?"

"None of your business."

"Because your ex is a firefighter?"

"......!"

Her brows jumped.

"So what?" she snapped, scowling at him.

"If you're still in love, why'd you break up?"

"Ask Yuuma."

With that, Saki walked away. She wasn't about to stop again, and he didn't consider stopping her.

Sakuta watched until she was out of sight, then stepped into the phone booth by the gates.

He lifted the receiver and inserted some coins into the green machine.

Naturally, he dialed Ikumi's number.

Saki had said she couldn't get in touch.

He hoped that was all in her head.

Just poor timing or a missed connection. He really didn't need any further problems.

But his faint hope was scattered by the mechanical message on the line.

"The number you have dialed is not in service. Please check the number and try again."

Just to be sure, he checked the number in his head and dialed once more.

But the outcome didn't change.

He put the phone down. There was a click, and his change was returned.

"What happened to Akagi?"

Was this reality being rewritten again?

He wasn't sure.

But if it was, his solution was unchanged.

The ball was in Miori's court.

He had no other means to restore this broken world.

Pinning his hopes on their Saturday excursion, he grabbed his change and left the phone booth.

Chapter
4
Two Lines Running Along,
Never Crossing

1

Saturday, April 8.

That morning, Sakuta was woken by the sound of rainfall outside. He crawled out of bed and parted the curtains, feeling gloomy. This was no April shower.

"Perfect day for a drive," he grumbled, feeling grayer than the clouds above.

He hauled himself to the living room, where he found Kaede in panda pajamas, getting breakfast ready.

When she spotted him, she called, "Good morning, Sakuta!" with a cheery smile.

On the table was the usual breakfast, and two stuffed lunch boxes. She must have been cooling them down before putting the lids on.

"You made lunches?"

"I'm a third-year in high school now, so I can handle this much before breakfast!"

"But it's a Saturday."

"The Animal Club is going to the zoo to see the pandas!"

"Hence the lunches. Wow. You're even making crab cream croquettes?" he asked, peering in.

The oblong croquettes were resting on a bed of lettuce.

"Those are frozen."

"And these tasty-looking chicken nuggets?"

He pointed to the next dish over.

"Delicious frozen food!"

"And the rolled eggs?"

"I made those!"

"Can't wait for lunch."

"It'll be great!"

Kaede was certainly a morning person. She left at eight, all eager and excited.

"I'm outta here, Sakuta!"

"Say hi to the pandas for me."

Kaede was in her Minegahara uniform, going to high school. She'd said she wanted to go to the same school he had—and now she was, keeping busy with her club.

Even if this was an illusion conjured up by Adolescence Syndrome, he couldn't help but have feelings about the reality before him. It made him feel all warm and fuzzy. And he knew those emotions were real, so he couldn't pretend they weren't happening.

Once Kaede was off to the zoo, Sakuta did the dishes and took care of the laundry. He cleaned up Nasuno's litter box and brushed her fur.

He still had plenty of time before he'd agreed to meet Miori, so he took the schedule planner out of the rucksack he used for college and sat down at the living room table, scowling at the syllabi.

First, he put down everything required, then began filling in the gaps with electives. And he added in classes required to get a teaching license.

This killed a shocking amount of time, and before he knew it, the clock showed eleven AM.

He ate an early lunch—every bite of the box Kaede had made for him. He changed clothes in his room, grabbed an umbrella, and went out.

The rain had died down a bit but was still a steady drizzle.

With the rain drumming on his umbrella, Sakuta walked to Fujisawa Station, avoiding the puddles.

He went through the JR gates to the platform below. About the same size crowd was waiting in either direction.

The inbound train came first, and Sakuta got on, then got off a station later at Ofuna.

He went up the stairs and out the biggest set of gates. This was within the range of the pass he'd bought for school—handy.

He looked around for Miori, but there was no sign of her.

Not wanting to get in the way, he moved to the side of the green booth.

Foot traffic was relatively light. There was still a decent number of passengers disembarking when a train pulled in, but at this hour, the station was never too crowded to meet up with people.

He'd know if Miori showed.

The clock had almost hit twelve.

The needle moved, and it was officially noon.

No Miori.

"……"

He checked the station exit, left, then right.

Miori had not arrived.

He checked the right exit—the east side of the station—once more, then the left exit—the west side.

While he repeated that, time marched on.

It was now 12:05.

Still no Miori.

Ten minutes passed, fifteen, twenty.

When the clock showed 12:25, Sakuta briefly left the south gate and headed for a different exit around the outside of the station.

He went up the stairs to the north gates, but no signs of Miori.

Just to be extra sure, he checked the gates of the Shonan Monorail, too.

All he'd actually said was *"Meet me at the gates of Ofuna Station."* He'd hoped she was just waiting at a different exit. It did seem oddly plausible that Miori might deliberately go wait at the monorail gates instead.

But sadly, she was nowhere near the Shonan Monorail.

Shrugging, Sakuta went back to the main exit, to the south.

She was already forty minutes late.

"Maybe she's not coming."

This was certainly beyond running "a little behind."

Best to assume this was deliberate. Intentional.

Potentially, he could wait all day, and she'd never show.

Aware of that possibility, Sakuta decided to tough it out.

By this point, he'd been waiting at Ofuna Station for well over an hour.

It was now 1:26.

He'd given up on scanning his surroundings.

He was just staring into space.

Another ten minutes went by…

"Wow, he's still here."

A wooden line reading from close at hand.

Sakuta turned toward the voice.

The very person he'd been waiting for had finally arrived. She wore a military jacket over a collared dress. Her hair was loosely half-up, like she'd just gotten out of the bath. As he took in her usual bored expression, Sakuta could see himself reflected in her eyes.

"You know, Mitou."

"What?"

"Is that really what you say after showing up an hour and thirty-six minutes late?"

"Sorry, I just wasn't sure what to wear," she explained, sounding like a girlfriend late to a date. "But who waits that long? I was just here to make sure you'd already left."

"Mai waited an hour and thirty-eight minutes for our first date."

"What the hell were you doing?"

"Exchanging butt kicks with a high school girl and getting yelled at by the police."

"That's preposterous," Miori cackled.

Her laugh always seemed like she was having fun.

And didn't let anyone else get closer.

"Azusagawa," she said, lining up next to him.

"What?"

"You want me to come forward, right? Tell everyone I'm the real Touko Kirishima?"

Her eyes were on the station crowds.

"If you don't, Mai really will become her."

"Everyone seems happy about it. It's all good."

"It's not good," he insisted.

"But it's not hurting anyone."

Miori wasn't backing down.

"If Mai's workload gets any worse, I'll never get to flirt with her."

"Ah-ha. That is a serious concern," she said, sounding not the least bit concerned.

"Mitou, are you cool with it?"

"Cool with what?"

"With Mai stealing Touko Kirishima from you."

Sakuta looked her right in the eye, and she shifted her gaze—but without a trace of awkwardness.

"Touko loved Mai. She'd be delighted."

It didn't sound like she was making excuses.

But it also didn't sound like she really meant it.

"Then is this what you sang for?"

"……"

"It isn't."

"First, can I ask one thing?"

"What?"

"Weren't we supposed to take a drive?"

"I've got a rental car reserved."

They could talk more in the car.

Sakuta led the way away from the gates and toward the station's east exit.

At the rental shop, Sakuta began by apologizing for not picking up the car at his reservation time.

"Sorry, my girlfriend showed up late," he said, using Miori as an excuse.

She was waiting outside the shop, and when she saw him looking, she smiled and waved. She couldn't hear a word of this, yet she played his "girlfriend" perfectly.

He showed his license, ran through the standard explanations, and came away with the keys. A nimble little compact was waiting for them.

Sakuta got in the driver's seat, and Miori took the passenger side.

They pulled out of the rental lot and drove off down Ofuna Nishi-Kamakura Road. The Shonan Monorail ran overhead, and every now and then, they'd chase or pass each other. Sometimes it was pretty neck and neck, giving this drive an added thrill.

Even Miori said, "Wow, the monorail's right next to us!"

"You do much driving since you got your license?"

"Nope. Don't feel like it."

"Because your friend got hit by a car?"

"......"

Miori didn't answer. She just kept looking away from him, out the window.

For a while, they matched pace with the monorail.

The rain had stopped.

"Touko was always asking me the same thing."

"......"

"'Miori, I want you to sing the songs I write.'"

The car stopped at a red light.

The engine noise faded, leaving just the two of them in silence.

"But I always said no," she whispered.

"......"

Sakuta kept his eyes on the traffic light, saying nothing.

"She asked so much we had a fight about it."

"......"

"We didn't speak to each other for a full week. That was the first time something like that ever happened."

"......"

The light turned green.

Sakuta pulled out.

The scenery swept by on either side. Oncoming traffic zipped by.

Out of the corner of his eye, he could see Miori staring out the passenger window. From the driver's seat, he couldn't see the look on her face.

"We were supposed to make up that day."

"The day she died?"

"Yeah. Christmas Eve. Split a curry bun and be friends again."

Miori made a sound that was sort of like a laugh, sort of like a sigh.

She'd said too little for him to read the emotions behind it.

It might have been regret. Might have been grief. There was no way he could know for sure. The state of Miori's mind was unfathomable. He couldn't peer into those depths. Whatever truth lay within was beyond Sakuta's reach.

It even seemed like there might be no emotions here.

And that's why Sakuta couldn't figure out what to say.

Hands on the steering wheel, he found his lips moving on their own.

"Well, you could split a curry bun with me today."

He glanced over at her.

"I'm pretty hungry," she said, dodging him. "I could easily eat two."

"Then we'll buy four and split them. That still counts as splitting, right?" he said, not skipping a beat.

"Oh, you *are* obnoxious," Miori cackled.

No matter how much laughter filled the car, the distance between them never shrank. The more fun Miori seemed to be having, the more obvious that was to Sakuta. It was almost painfully clear.

They stopped by a store to buy four curry buns. Their order cleared out the store's stock.

They'd followed the monorail all the way to Nishi-Kamakura Station, but now they turned south and headed to the coast.

At Koshigoe, they turned onto Route 134 and drove along with the ocean on their right. They got pretty close to Kamakura, then turned back, like they wanted a second helping of that view.

Currently, they were in the parking lot at Shichirigahama.

Sakuta and Miori were out of the car, walking along the beach.

They were enjoying their curry buns.

"Watch out for kites."

Three birds of prey wheeled overhead. There was a distinct possibility those birds were aiming to swipe their food.

"The surf's pretty loud," Miori said.

It was unusually powerful. Enough to drown out anything said softly.

Enoshima was on their right.

On a clear day, they'd have seen Mount Fuji in the distance.

But today was cloudy, so there was no sign of it.

Fortunately, the recent rain had stopped.

Sakuta focused on getting the curry bun in his belly before the kites won. He'd bought some bottled tea with it and took a sip, then stared off at the horizon three miles away.

At last he spoke.

"When I was in my third year of junior high, my sister—she's two years younger than me—was targeted by some bullies. She wound up developing Adolescence Syndrome."

Miori was walking two, three steps away. She glanced his way.

"Her classmates' words cut into her skin like knives. Her Adolescence Syndrome drew actual blood, or left bruises… No one believed me. Not her teachers, not her classmates, no one."

"……"

Miori said nothing. But kept her eyes on him.

"I didn't want anything to do with those assholes. I came down here and threw my phone into the ocean."

His voice was raised a bit, fighting with the wind and surf.

"You really shouldn't throw your trash in the water."

"Mai said the roughly same thing. 'You should really use a trash can.'"

A lot of time had passed since then.

"Should I assume you got rid of your phone because you think your text caused Touko Kirishima's accident?" Sakuta asked.

"No," she snapped.

"Then why?"

"Because everyone at school knew how close we were. They kept hounding me with texts. 'Are you okay?' 'Cheer up!' 'I'm here for you.' I got sick of it and ditched my phone."

"That's very you."

"I know," Miori said, satisfied.

"If the guys were worried about you, that would make some girls jealous."

"I am that bitch."

She acknowledged his point and laughed at herself. She often smiled in a way that seemed slightly uneasy.

"So, Mitou."

"Mm-hmm?"

"You asked me the other day if I'd ever killed anyone."

"And?"

"I have."

"Call the police!"

"My second year of high school, on December twenty-fourth…I was supposed to die."

"……?"

Miori turned to look at him, a faint gleam of interest in her eyes. He could tell that he had her attention now, so he pressed on.

"A car slipped on the ice at the crossing by Enoshima and should have run me over."

"......"

"When I failed to wake up, my heart would have been transplanted into a junior high school girl."

"Then am I talking to a ghost right now?"

Miori laughed at her own question. It clearly wasn't true.

"We changed the future. With Adolescence Syndrome. Redid things to arrive at a new possibility."

"......"

Sakuta looked her right in the eye. He wanted Miori to know he was telling the truth. She had to believe him.

Miori held his gaze. She blinked several times. It took her time to chew this over. He could tell she was.

"What happened to the girl who should have received your heart?"

Her first question got right to the crux of the matter.

"She found a different donor and is doing just fine."

"Ah," Miori murmured, nodding. "And her donor was Touko," she added, half to herself.

"Mm," Sakuta said. He nodded, slowly and emphatically. "So it might be my fault Touko Kirishima died."

"......"

Sakuta met Miori's gaze head-on.

He forgot to blink.

Neither moved. It was like time had stopped.

The silence lasted less than ten seconds.

But it felt like an eternity.

Eventually, Miori's gaze dropped a bit.

"Is this a story about you pulling another do-over and saving Touko?" she asked, her voice flat. No hopes, no expectations. There was simply a serious expression on her face, which made her teardrop mole stand out.

"I've been told that's not in the cards. We can go back from the future to the present, but not from the present to the past."

That alone would hardly explain it. And he was sure it wouldn't be very convincing.

But for some reason, he was sure the only thing Miori needed to hear was the conclusion.

She didn't need the theory or the logic, just the facts.

"Then why tell me at all?"

There was no trace of disappointment. Just getting to the point.

Verifying Sakuta's motives. Her eyes on him again.

"Isn't it obvious?"

"Is it?"

"You can't be friends if you're keeping secrets."

"I'm pretty sure I made my intentions clear the other day."

Miori picked up a little shell from the beach. Half a bivalve. She played with it in her hand.

"When Touko died, I wasn't the least bit sad," she muttered. "Didn't cry at all."

"……"

Even now, there were no tears. Her voice wasn't choked up.

"I was like, 'She's dead? What the hell?'"

She was the same old Miori.

"I went to the funeral, then I went to class without her, and it didn't feel real. Part of me expected to see her again the next day."

It sounded as though she still felt that way.

"But you never did."

"Yeah. And the next Christmas rolled around. By that point, no one was talking about Touko anymore."

"……"

"So I thought I should sing the songs Touko left behind. She'd wanted me to sing them. I uploaded the first song on the anniversary of her death."

December 24. Christmas Eve.

"It did shockingly well," Miori said, placing the shell at the edge of the surf. "And I had more songs by her."

On the wet sand, the shell was soon grabbed by the waves and washed away. Off to somewhere else. Like how Touko had left her.

"I put them out there, one at a time."

Miori's eyes were on the ocean.

"So many people said, 'I love Touko Kirishima.'"

On the horizon.

"They talked about 'Touko Kirishima.'"

Sakuta felt like Miori's words were directed at nobody.

"But that wasn't the Touko I wanted to see."

"……"

"No matter how many songs I sang, it didn't bring her to me."

"Is that why you stopped?"

"I also ran out of songs. I put the last one out on Christmas Eve, a year after I started."

"And yet Touko Kirishima songs kept showing up."

"I really didn't see that coming."

Multiple people started claiming to be Touko Kirishima, singing as her.

Miori mustered a guilty smile.

But it soon gave way to her usual one, her eyes on the horizon again.

"Azusagawa."

"What?"

"Do you still want to be friends with a heartless girl who doesn't shed a tear over a friend's death?"

"I do."

"Really?"

"What about you?"

"Me?"

Miori turned to face him. His face was reflected in her eyes.

"I might have caused your friend's death," he said. "Does that rule out us being friends?"

"……What do I even want?"

It was an evasive response. Her eyes fled to the water. A very Miori way to avoid the issue.

But it also felt genuine.

The ocean surface wasn't gleaming, but she squinted at it anyway. As if searching for the shape of her own emotions.

If she really was just trying to brush him off, she'd have found a more effective means.

"I just want to see Touko again."

Her voice was so soft the wind and surf nearly drowned it out.

And again, it sounded like she was speaking from the heart.

"Is that why you rewrote reality, Mitou?"

"……Around the time I stopped singing, I started waking up in the morning and found things a little bit different."

"……"

"The curtains would be a lighter shade of blue. My favorite cat mug would have a dog on the side instead. I'd have a different teacher."

"Was that what you wanted?"

She neither nodded nor shook her head.

Instead…

"If reality's being rewritten, I wanted one where Touko was still alive. Too bad, I guess."

Her tone never changed.

"Why the past tense? Don't you still want that?"

"My reality stopped being rewritten a while back."

"When…?"

"Last fall. When I met you at that core curriculum party, Azusagawa."

"……"

He had not expected his name to come up here, and he blinked at her, visibly confused.

Miori clearly appreciated that reaction.

"What did you do to me?" she asked.

"You sound sure I'm the cause."

"It was my first time meeting an Azusagawa without a phone."

"Sounds like you met a lot of other me's."

"I did. An Azusagawa who wore glasses, one who was in med school—one was super slick. I was curious about Mai's boyfriend, so I went up to you each time reality was rewritten. I must have met at least fifty versions."

"Did any of them become your friend?"

"Not a single one."

"Then I'm gonna be the first. What an honor."

"If that happens." Miori made it sound like she was just a bystander. They were hollow, empty words. "So there you have it, Azusagawa."

"Have what?"

"Any way you can arrange it so I can find a reality where Touko's alive?"

"In return, will you come forward as the real Touko Kirishima?"

"Should we pinkie promise?"

She held up her little finger.

"Nah. I trust you," he said.

"Oh, you *are* obnoxious!" she said, laughing merrily.

Still smiling, she said, "I've got a shift, so I'd better go."

She waved goodbye.

"We've got the car. I'll drop you off."

"I work right there."

"Right where?"

"The café by the parking lot."

Miori turned her back on the water and walked away. She went up the stairs by the breakwater. Sakuta silently watched her go.

They each followed their own line. Their paths led them straight ahead, never crossing. That was the current state of their relationship.

2

Sakuta got the rental car back to Ofuna before five. He returned the car, got on the Tokaido Line, and rode back to Fujisawa.

That took less than five minutes.

He followed other passengers out onto the platform, went up the stairs, and tapped his pass on the gates. His feet took him to the north exit, but rather than go home, he headed for the cram school near the station.

Sakuta didn't have any classes today, but at this hour on a Saturday, he figured Rio would be there. He wanted to ask her about Miori.

As he neared the building, he found someone very tall by the elevators.

Toranosuke Kasai.

This boy was nearly six foot three.

"Self-study?" Sakuta asked.

"Mm? Oh, Azusagawa-sensei. Basically, yeah. I wanted to review the mock test."

The elevator arrived, and they got on.

Toranosuke hit the button. The elevator started moving, and he let out a long sigh.

"Not feeling it?"

"I'm doing all right."

"Test results not so good?"

"Pretty bad."

"So the dream came true," Sakuta muttered.

"……?" Toranosuke frowned at him.

Like Tomoe and Sara, he didn't remember the dreaming hashtag.

"Well, the real thing's still almost a year off. Don't let it get to you. Spring of my third year, my mock exam was straight-up awful."

"Right…"

Clearly, he wasn't doing okay. He seemed barely there at all.

One step inside the cram school, and it became obvious this wasn't just about the mock test.

As the doors opened, Toranosuke called a greeting to the teachers' area.

Sakuta followed after him, but the boy pulled up short, and he nearly ran into him.

"Erp…what?"

He leaned around, getting a look at Toranosuke's face. His eyes were locked on something between the free space and the teachers' area.

Sara was at the counter, asking Rio a question. She was diligently answering, pointing at something in their notes. Toranosuke's eyes were on Rio, and he seemed even more serious than she was.

"Must be tough falling for the girlfriend of a senpai from your basketball team."

Reality had been rewritten, but Toranosuke's feelings for her had not changed. If anything, the changes to Rio and Yuuma's relationship had made things quite a bit messier.

"I don't… Futaba-sensei's just…"

He stammered a denial, but there wasn't much force behind it.

"Thanks so much, Rio-sensei!" Sara said, snapping her notes closed. At this point they both noticed Sakuta and Toranosuke.

"I'm off to the self-study rooms," the latter said, and he made himself scarce.

A moment later, Sara came over.

"Sakuta-sensei, do you even have a class? Yamada and Yoshiwa were talking about hitting Kamakura today."

"I'm here for Futaba."

"I'm about to teach Himeji."

Rio stepped out of the teachers' area, unperturbed.

"I'll wait till you're done."

"Once it's over, I'm meeting Kunimi for dinner."

"What time?"

"Eight."

It was six. Classes were eighty minutes, so she'd wrap up at 7:20.

"Gimme those forty minutes."

"……I'll hear you out, at least."

She didn't seem particularly motivated. The polar opposite of that.

He could guess why.

"Thanks," he said.

Sara watched with interest, but Sakuta pretended not to notice.

3

When Sakuta finished telling Rio everything, their coffee cups were both empty.

They were at the counter in an awfully fancy café near the cram school. Through the glass windows, they had a great view of the foot traffic outside.

This place had a liquor license, and a couple in their midtwenties toward the back were laughing a bit too loudly. They must have been regulars; the shop staff were yukking it up with them.

"That's about everything I've been through the last few days."

Mai claiming to be Touko Kirishima, hiragana Kaede waiting for him at home, all kinds of other changes, and the discovery that the real Touko Kirishima was long since dead. And that she turned out to be Shouko's donor. Finally, that Miori Mitou from college was the real singer going by the Touko Kirishima name.

"What do you make of it?"

Rio had listened in silence, but now she sighed. Her gaze was on the crowd outside, but not really looking.

"You've said a lot of things I find hard to believe, but accepting it all for the moment—what do you *want* to do?"

Rio sounded like she was testing him.

"Good question."

"Do you want Sakurajima-senpai back?"

"Well, obviously."

Arguably his primary purpose.

"Or do you want to make amends to Miori Mitou and Touko Kirishima?"

"……"

He didn't have a ready answer for that one. Sakuta shifted his gaze from Rio's face to the street.

"I don't think I have any guilt where Mitou's concerned."

He wasn't sure changing the future had caused Touko's accident. Not if he understood Rio's explanation of the butterfly effect.

"Then what do you think?"

He thought about that, then reached the same conclusion.

"I think I wanna be her friend."

Not just the surface meaning of the word. *Friend* didn't mean the same thing as it had before finding out Touko was Shouko's donor. But *friend* was still the only word he had to describe his relationship with Miori.

"Do you want to change back everything that's been rewritten?"

Rio had imbued her last question with a very meaningful tone. It was impossible to miss the drop in temperature. Sakuta was sure it wasn't just in his head.

There was a hint of tension in her voice. The air around them crackled.

He didn't have to wonder why.

If everything went back to normal, Rio's life would be reset. Rio and Yuuma would be just friends again, no longer dating.

So Sakuta left that question unanswered and asked a question of his own.

"If Mitou keeps rewriting things, do you think she'll eventually find a reality where Touko Kirishima is alive?"

"I do not."

Rio didn't really hesitate.

"Your reasoning?"

"Most of the changes you perceive relate to the #dreaming posts from before the rewrite happened."

That much was pretty clear.

"True, there were dreams about Mai claiming to be Touko Kirishima, and about both Kaedes, and about you and Kunimi."

And Toranosuke's bad mock exam, and Kento and Juri getting closer.

"And before reality was rewritten, I told you what those dreams were."

"Visions of another potential world."

Rio nodded.

"We have to assume these dreams allowed someone to perceive those possibilities and they made that a reality."

"In other words, unless someone dreamed that Touko Kirishima was alive, then there's no way to rewrite reality the way Mitou wants?"

"She's the one who should be dreaming about Touko Kirishima."

"Yeah."

If that was what Miori wanted.

"In which case, she doesn't *really* want to see her again," Rio said.

A sudden one-eighty.

But not a surprise.

"……"

Sakuta found himself agreeing, and that made his face tense up.

"I see you've worked that out, Azusagawa."

Something about Miori's manner had put the idea in his head.

And if Rio was pointing out the same thing, he couldn't dismiss that idea.

"Adolescence Syndrome mostly *does* grant the wish of the person who has it," he said.

"Exactly."

"Mitou says she wants to see Touko Kirishima, yet she hasn't."

"Maybe she's running away."

"From Touko Kirishima?"

Rio nodded, eyes on her hands.

"Or at least from Touko Kirishima's death."

Miori's behavior had suggested that much. It was hard to get a read on her, hard to tell where her heart lay—and that had given Sakuta this impression.

They fell silent. And Rio's phone vibrated on the table.

She glanced at it.

"Kunimi?"

"Mm. He's almost here."

Inside of a minute, they saw his face outside. Yuuma spotted them through the window and waved.

Rio got up.

"Look, Azusagawa," she said, not looking at him.

"Yeah?" he replied, keeping his eyes on Yuuma.

"This is as far as I go."

She made that very clear.

"It's plenty."

Sakuta tried to smile but failed.

He knew where this was going, so he couldn't manage it.

"I like it better this way," Rio said while watching Yuuma come to the door. He was smiling happily, unaware that anything might be out of the ordinary. For him, it was just another fun evening.

"I'm going," Rio said, not waiting for Sakuta to answer.

She joined Yuuma at the door, and they headed off toward the station. Yuuma turned back once, waving a hand at Sakuta.

The portrait of happiness.

And it sure tugged at his heartstrings.

4

Sakuta sat for a while after Rio and Yuuma left. When he finally exited the café, he made his way out of the brightly lit station area and onto the road he'd walked nearly every day.

He took his time and reflected on Rio's words.

——*"I like it better this way."*

Seeing her with Yuuma had made him realize he felt the same way. And awareness of that slowed him down. He wanted to sort out his feelings before he got home. And that made him stretch out the time of his commute.

What was normally a ten-minute walk took him twenty.

He arrived at the building and still didn't have his thoughts straight. If anything, they were in more turmoil.

He got on the elevator, his brain spinning.

By the time he opened the door and said, "I'm home," *"I like it better"* was still echoing through his mind.

"Sakuta, welcome back!" Kaede said, coming out to greet him.

Only then did he pull himself out of the spiral.

"I told the pandas hi for you!"

She'd accomplished the mission he'd set for her.

When he saw her innocent smile, he found himself asking, "Do you like it better this way?"

"What are we talking about?" she asked, tilting her head. She went so far that her whole body tilted with it.

"Nothing, never mind."

He took off his shoes, then stepped into the apartment.

"I want to be with my brother forever!"

Not an unusual statement. Kaede said things like this. But her smile was so dazzling it lit a fire inside him. The heat raced through his body, gathering behind his eyes.

"……"

"Sakuta?"

He found himself on the verge of tears.

The only thing that stopped them from spilling over was the ringing of the phone.

He headed to the living room.

The display showed Shouko's number.

"I'll get it," he told Kaede, picking up. "Azusagawa speaking."

"Sakuta? It's me, Shouko."

"I was planning on calling you. About Mitou."

"Then wanna meet now?"

"Now?"

He checked the clock. It was half past eight.

"There's something I want you to see."

She sounded serious. Calm, but insistent. This must be important.

"Okay," Sakuta said.

His voice carried through the phone line.

He met Shouko at the same Fujisawa Station restaurant where he worked part-time. When he went inside, he found her waiting in a booth by the windows, waving at him.

The place was only half-full, a slow-paced evening. Sakuta ordered the drink bar only and sat down across from Shouko.

"Thanks for waiting."

"Don't worry, I only just got here."

"So what did you want to show me?"

"……"

When he got right down to business, Shouko gave him an odd look.

"What?"

"What happened to you, Sakuta?"

"Meaning?"

"It's not like you to just ignore a classic date line."

"……"

He had to wince at that one.

"Earlier, Futaba told me she likes it better this way," he admitted, figuring it wasn't worth hiding.

"……I can see how that would get under your skin."

"I went home, and Kaede was waiting for me…and I kinda get where Futaba's coming from."

Tomoe going to his school, Uzuki still attending classes—neither was exactly bad for him. Both were actually welcome changes.

"In which case, do you want to leave it alone?"

"I've gotta get Mai back to her old self."

The rest was a tough choice. There were pros and cons. Some he couldn't choose.

Shouko seemed satisfied with that answer, and she moved on.

"Did you have a good talk with Miori? You went on a drive date, right?"

"Mitou said she wanted to see Touko Kirishima again. But when I relayed that to Futaba, she suggested it's the opposite."

"She doesn't want to see her?"

"I don't know why Mitou would feel that way, but situationally…"

"In that case, I'm glad I called you today."

"Mm?"

"This is what I wanted to show you."

Shouko pulled Touko and Miori's exchange diary out of her bag. The one Touko's mother had given her. She placed it on the table and flipped through the pages.

And stopped when she found the right one.

The date on it read December 24.

"The day Touko Kirishima died?"

"Yes, that Christmas Eve."

Sakuta felt like he recognized the writing.

On closer inspection, it was the lyrics to a Touko Kirishima song.

The one Mai sang onstage on April 1.

I'm glad I met you.
That's not how I see things.
My soulmate's no longer out there.
But the love songs we listened to all agree.
We will meet again.
Don't be afraid to get lost.
Get up, fling that door open, step outside.
But the future's not guaranteed.
I'll be alone again tomorrow.
No one to split things with.
This empty hollow in my heart.
If I have to feel like this...
I wish I'd never met you.

Below the lyrics was the song title: "Turn the World Upside Down."

That was the last entry in the exchange diary. All pages after it were blank.

"This was Touko Kirishima's entry?"

"I'm sure of it. They have pretty different handwriting."

Miori's letters were sharp and angular, while Touko's were rounded.

"Mitou said she was supposed to meet Touko Kirishima that day. They'd had a fight the week before and were gonna make up."

"But Touko was in an accident on the way to see Miori."

"Yeah."

"So in Miori's mind, these lyrics were Touko's last words."

Shouko tapped the final line of the song.

"……'I wish I'd never met you.'"

"Exactly."

"That's a pretty good reason for her to be running. If your best friend said that, it's gotta hurt."

"But I think she's reading that wrong," Shouko argued.

"How so?" Sakuta asked, not sure what she meant.

"There's something I have to tell Miori about these lyrics."

"……"

"Sakuta," Shouko said, looking him right in the eye.

He already knew what she was about say next, so he chose to remain silent.

"Bring me to Miori Mitou."

I'm glad I met you.

NEXT TIME...

...THE SERIES CONCLUSION!

Rascal DOES NOT DREAM of a Dear Friend

Hajime Kamoshida

Illustration by
Keji Mizoguchi

On sale in 2025!

Getting closer to the truth about Miori and Touko Kirishima means a choice will have to be made.

Sakuta faces the final Adolescence Syndrome as Volume 15 concludes the *Rascal* series!

HAVE YOU BEEN TURNED ON TO LIGHT NOVELS YET?

86—EIGHTY-SIX, VOL. 1-13

In truth, there is no such thing as a bloodless war. Beyond the fortified walls protecting the eighty-five Republic Sectors lies the "nonexistent" Eighty-Sixth Sector. The young men and women of this forsaken land are branded the Eighty-Six and, stripped of their humanity, pilot "unmanned" weapons into battle...

Manga adaptation available now!

WOLF & PARCHMENT, VOL. 1-10

The young man Col dreams of one day joining the holy clergy and departs on a journey from the bathhouse, Spice and Wolf. Winfiel Kingdom's prince has invited him to help correct the sins of the Church. But as his travels begin, Col discovers in his luggage a young girl with a wolf's ears and tail named Myuri, who stowed away for the ride!

Manga adaptation available now!

SOLO LEVELING, VOL. 1-8

E-rank hunter Jinwoo Sung has no money, no talent, and no prospects to speak of—and apparently, no luck, either! When he enters a hidden double dungeon one fateful day, he's abandoned by his party and left to die at the hands of some of the most horrific monsters he's ever encountered.

Comic adaptation available now!

THE SAGA OF TANYA THE EVIL, VOL. 1-14

Reborn as a destitute orphaned girl with nothing to her name but memories of a previous life, Tanya will do whatever it takes to survive, even if it means living life behind the barrel of a gun!

Manga adaptation available now!

SO I'M A SPIDER, SO WHAT?, VOL. 1-16

I used to be a normal high school girl, but in the blink of an eye, I woke up in a place I've never seen before and—and I was reborn as a spider?!

Manga adaptation available now!

OVERLORD, VOL. 1-16

When Momonga logs in one last time just to be there when the servers go dark, something happens—and suddenly, fantasy is reality. A rogues' gallery of fanatically devoted NPCs is ready to obey his every order, but the world Momonga now inhabits is not the one he remembers.

Manga adaptation available now!

VISIT YENPRESS.COM TO CHECK OUT ALL OUR TITLES AND...

GET YOUR YEN ON!